THE
SERPENT LORD

*For Kathy, Nancy, Rick,
Wendy and Marc.
We started out life together.*

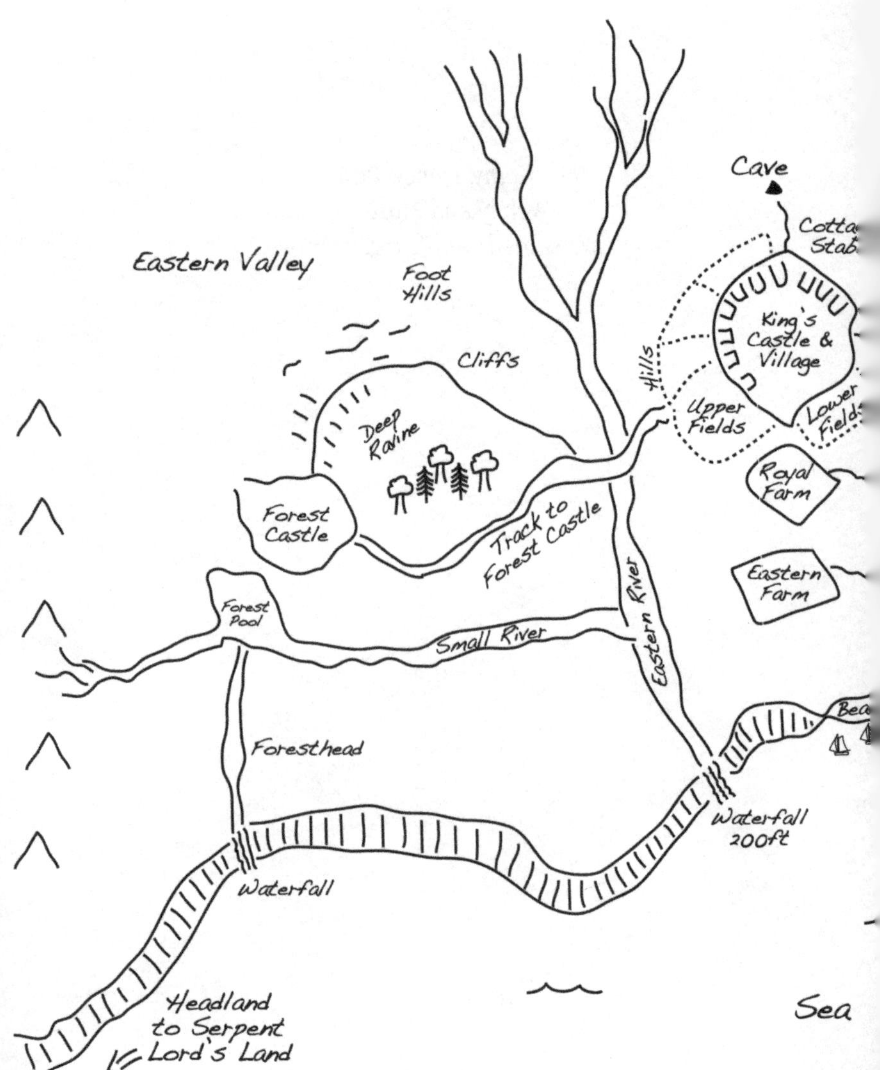
The Kingdom of the Three Valleys
Mountains
10-18 thousand ft
Cave
Cotta
Stab
King's Castle & Village
Eastern Valley
Foot Hills
Cliffs
Hills
Upper Fields
Lower Fields
Deep Ravine
Royal Farm
Forest Castle
Track to Forest Castle
Eastern Farm
Forest Pool
Small River
Eastern River
Foresthead
Bea
Waterfall 200ft
Waterfall
Headland to Serpent Lord's Land
Sea

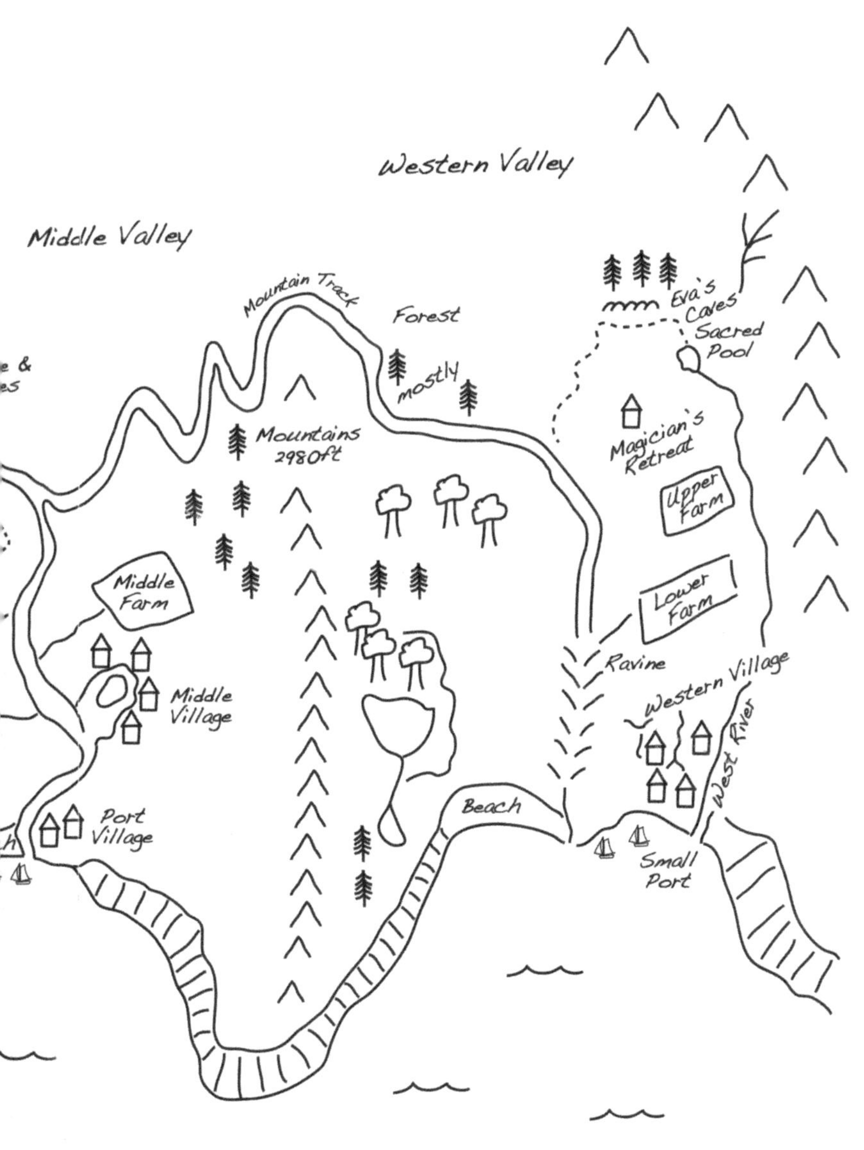

Western Valley
Middle Valley
Mountain Track
Forest
mostly
Eva's Caves
Sacred Pool
Magician's Retreat
Upper Farm
Mountains 2980ft
Lower Farm
e &
es
Middle Farm
Ravine
Western Village
West River
Middle Village
Port Village
Beach
Small Port
h

THE
SERPENT LORD

By E. M. Scott

Published under licence by Brown Dog Books
and The Self Publishing Partnership
7 Green Park Station, Bath BA1 1JB

www.selfpublishingpartnership.co.uk

ISBN printed book: 978-1-78545-131-7
ISBN e-book: 978-1-78545-132-4

Cover design by Kevin Rylands
Internal design by Andrew Easton
Illustrations by David Powell

Printed and bound by
CPI Group (UK) Ltd, Croydon CR0 4YY

East is west and west is east
in the reflection of our minds.

Prologue

The sky was lightening above the silhouette of the mountains. Adela stood on the path at the eastern side of the Forest Castle. Under the golden bracken beside her slept the wolves. Ebony and Dawn, Lola had named them. Adela tried to run her hands over their thickening coats, but she could not feel with her hands. The senses of sight and hearing were still hers, but physical sensation had left with her old body, which now rested in the simple grave nearby. The wolves kept watch over it by night.

The wolves, though, could feel Adela's affections. Dawn stretched and sat up-right, her coat shuddering a little from the feeling of Adela's stroke. She turned and faced the rising sun over the now snowy peaks, along with her ethereal mistress. The forest was recovering from the enchantment cast by the serpents in the well. The green mists had continued to lift from the moment Lola had bound the serpents with the sacred words given to her by Adela in a dream. Autumn was emerging and, with the quickening light, showed off the yellows and golds of the oak leaves.

This was not how Adela remembered her start as the new Forest Queen. Her predecessor had gently slipped away three nights before the longest day. There had been a simple burial ceremony. Then, on the longest day, Adela and all of the other un-promised young women near to her own age were gathered together with the King, The Magician and everyone who lived nearby. They watched as the ancient yew tree folded in on itself upon their arrival. Then, she and four others were called forth.

Now, at the end of her reign, Adela felt the on-coming winter, but she had no heir. A successor could only be chosen on the shortest or longest day. And the serpents, the serpents had always been there, but they had never been as strong as they were when they took her life from her. Had they been as strong at the end of the last Forest Queen's reign?

Dear Lola, Adela thought. If it had not been for her, the Three Valleys would have been lost along with all that they protected. How could they be kept safe now?

Adela looked towards the eastern sky. There were small clouds passing on a gentle breeze over the forest. Adela raised her arms and then swirled around. The clouds began to move together and became darker. Yes, she could still provide some defense to the east.

Adela stroked Dawn's head. *"Best take cover dear one, we are in for a storm."*

CHAPTER 1

An Arrow

Benu flicked one triangular ear back. The hairs inside always tickled his forehead when he did this. His whiskers twitched as a result. Isis rolled away from him. She was having such a lovely dream chasing a red squirrel up the holly-oak tree that guarded Eva's retreat. Eva would have told her off if she had been there, but she wasn't. Eva was far away, watching water crash on rocks at the big wet open space, a place Isis had never been to.

"Intruder," said Benu as he sat up.

As the male of the household he saw it as his responsibility to warn Eva or Isis of any danger. He took life far more seriously than Isis did.

"Dog, no wolf. Come," he said as he gracefully leapt over Isis and off the high platform bed that they shared with Eva. It was always colder without Eva; she would make a fire in the little stove in the corner of the cave. Benu's exit made Isis feel the draft.

"M-m-m, do I have to? The fox will be there." Isis moaned as she rolled towards the door opening and looked out. She didn't want to move from the spot where their two bodies had built up warmth.

"Now!" said Benu, *"I can smell blood."*

Isis jumped down onto the floor and stretched out both back legs at the same time. Her silver fur caught a sparkle of moonlight from the small window by the bed. She poked her head out of the flap in the door. Benu had already scrambled up the pole to the top of the awning fixed to the entrance of the cave.

"Up Isis," he said, *"this could be dangerous."*

Isis leapt and jumped and was beside Benu in an instant. *"The fox is near, but hiding,"* she said.

"Yes, and we are all downwind of the wolf, not good," Benu warned.

A gentle breeze was filtering over the top of the cliffs towards the caves. The wolf would be able to smell them all. The cats heard the shifting of some pebbles and then a whine. Benu could now see the wolf's eyes. His hair stood on end, puffing out his thick white and tabby coat to make him look three times his real size. Isis did the same. Her hair was much finer and didn't enlarge her quite so much, but she still looked bigger.

The wolf came closer. It was limping.

"A she-wolf, injured," whispered Isis.

"Benu, Isis." Eva's voice came to them through a broken whine. *"It's me."* The wolf collapsed. Then its limbs started to shift and change.

"Eva, Eva hurt." Benu jumped down in one movement and was at his mistress's side, licking her face and finding the source of the smell of blood. *"Find the fox,"* he said to Isis, *"so she can lick the wound."*

Benu and Isis knew that cat saliva was toxic to human wounds, but canine wasn't.

"I thought you were coming back as a seagull," Benu sent to Eva.

"Seagulls are considered food for someone down on the beach. I had to travel back as a wolf, but the wound didn't disappear with the change. It is a gash from an arrow on my front leg rather than my wing." Eva was trying to sit up as she explained her injury.

The fox appeared now, sniffing and wanting to lick Eva's wound.

"It's alright, Tara, I can make it to the water." Eva got up and stumbled towards a large barrel by the entrance to the next small cave, which was partially formed by a hut built into the cliff. She took a tin cup from a hook above the barrel and drank. The effect of the shape-shifting was wearing off, but not the exhaustion of travelling twelve miles up the mountain path on three legs. She poured water over the wound on her upper arm. Her right arm, the one she did everything with. Bad luck, she thought.

Eva took another drink. That would have to do for now. She stumbled back to her sleeping cave and opened the door. The bed was still warm where Benu and Isis had been sleeping. Sleep now, she thought as she climbed into her bed, still bleeding. Isis was beside her in seconds. Benu followed. Eva wrapped her sleeve tightly around the wound and then fell into a deep sleep.

The three settled down into their pattern of sleeping. Eva was in the middle with Isis by her left side. Benu stretched across the bottom of her right side. Eva had made the platform big enough to offer plenty of room for her and the two cats. She had found them as kittens, two forest kittens left on the edge of a field to fend for themselves. She had always had cats as companions. She had lost her old tabby, Duncan, only months before finding them. She had no idea if they were litter mates, and they couldn't recall either.

In the very depths of winter, sometimes the fox crawled into bed with them, but she usually kept company with her latest brood in a small cave above them on the next cliff.

Eva slept soundly, with Benu checking her every once in a while. She was exhausted so she didn't notice his turning over and prodding her.

The full moon had set. Light started to seep into the sky. Eva slept on.

The fox entered the cave at mid-morning. *"I'll watch, you hunt,"* she said.

At this Isis leapt off of the bed, but Benu still sat by Eva.

"Do you think we should tell the old man?" said Benu, reluctant to leave his mistress.

"If she hasn't risen by the time the sun is overhead, I'll go," replied Tara.

"Alright, I'll hunt, but I'll be back soon." Benu jumped down and followed after Isis.

Tara leapt up and sat beside Eva. She sniffed Eva's forehead. She could feel heat coming from it. Not good, she thought, humans should not have hot heads. She decided she should go for the old man as soon as the others got back.

Isis was the best hunter of the three. She managed a mouse for herself and one for Benu in less than half an hour and was soon back through the cat door, cleaning her whiskers.

"I'll go now," said Tara upon Isis' return. *"Stay with her, she's not good."*

Isis willingly rejoined her mistress on the bed, her favourite place in the whole world. Benu kept watch at the door as Tara disappeared down the mountain path.

* * * * * * * *

Pixey loved to chase the dust in the sunbeams as Lola swept. Lola was trying to look after The Magician as best she could now. She was beginning to understand that she would learn by watching and listening to his daily routines just as much as she would by formal instruction. She was also trying much harder to learn to read so she could look up spells and herbal remedies.

Since they had returned from the King's Middle Valley, The Magician had shown her how to use herbs to brew healing teas and medicines. He had also fully initiated her into the making of soup. Not magical soup, just nutritious, savoury and tasty soup. This was nothing to do with The Magician being a magician. It was a hobby of his. Soup filled and warmed one, from kings to the most ordinary field hand.

"Soup," proclaimed The Magician, "can be made from almost anything and satisfy the hunger of almost anyone. Therefore soup is an extremely important part of human existence."

This was said often in the cottage and made Lola giggle, but she could also see the truth in it. With the coming of winter, she was grateful for The Magician's culinary enthusiasm.

It was in the middle of preparing a carrot and pumpkin soup on his low oak kitchen table, that The Magician noticed Tara out of the window that faced into the woods. The fox sat and stared, then ran up the hill a few feet before returning back to her original spot.

Pixey was sitting on the top of The Magician's chair in the other side of the open room of the cottage. Lola had gone out the front door with the dust pan. Pixey was Lola's constant companion in cleaning up, except when it meant going out into the frost.

"*Ma's fox?*" she thought.

The Magician could understand many of Pixey's thoughts. "*No little one,*" he sent, "*but one we know.*" The Magician rinsed his hands of pumpkin meat in a small bowl of water. "Lola, I'm going up the mountain," he called as he dried his hands on his robe.

"*You don't bring me good news, do you little friend?*" he sent to the fox. "*What shall I bring?*"

Tara picked up his thoughts clearly. "*Eva, hot, bleeding, still sleeping,*" she sent back.

"M-m-m," The Magician opened his cupboard. He took out some sage, some of the mushrooms that he had collected from the forest of the Middle Valley and some of his very special honey. "That will have to do for now," he said to himself, "no doubt she'll have the other things I need."

The Magician put the items in a small leather satchel that he slung over his shoulder. "Lola, see what you can do with this soup. Remember what I taught you about the onions," he called out as he went out the back door of the cottage.

Lola appeared seconds later. She had heard very little of what he had said. *"Where's he gone?"* she sent to Pixey.

"With the fox. Not our fox, a different fox. Fast, faster than we ever go," replied Pixey, still looking out of the window. The Magician and the fox seemed to have disappeared in seconds.

The Magician quickly made his way up the mountain path. He had gone up to Eva's retreat a few days before to thank her for preparing the cottage on his return from the Middle Valley with Lola. The cats had explained that Eva had gone all the way down to the sea to investigate a small shipwreck that a young farmhand had told her about. As she was deputizing for The Magician, Eva thought it provident to find out what had happened sooner, rather than later when he returned.

When he needed to, The Magician would walk at a speed much faster than a human might expect to. He easily kept up with the scampering Tara who weaved her way through the rocks and roots of the forest floor.

They came to the holly-oak by midday. He could see the three small caves set into the side of the cliffs. But no smoke came out of the chimney at the side of the sleeping cave which was nearest the path. Eva always had a slow burning fire lit at this time of year.

"Breathing, but not moving," the fox explained as she scampered up the path.

The Magician quickly followed and was soon at the door of Eva's sleeping cave. The door was ajar. He gently pushed it open. There, collapsed on her bed with travelling clothes still on, lay Eva. Blood stained through her shirt on her right shoulder.

He went over and felt her forehead. It was hot and her wound was infected.

Eva stirred. "Ellery, I'm not so good I think," she murmured.

"No, but we'll get you better again".

The Magician put down his bag on a small pine table. He pulled out the honey, setting it ready. He then rummaged through the bag for another moment and pulled out a small pocket knife, hinged to a wooden cover. He cut along the sleeve of Eva's tunic to reveal a deep slice in her upper arm. The arrow had gone in deep, and then had been pulled roughly with the gull's beak.

"Not a clean wound Eva," he noted as he gently inspected it, "and becoming quite infected. I wonder what the arrow was made of."

"Some kind of slate I think, though I didn't recognise it," Eva said trying to clarify what she saw in her seagull's mind's eye. "The hunter had been on the beach for some time. She came out of a shelter made of driftwood and sail canvass. It was almost camouflaged from above, but when I fell the entrance was visible from across the beach."

"Shh, shh, not now," The Magician gently touched Eva's forehead. "Tell me in a day or two, you should rest."

"M-m…," Eva realised that she could not stay coherent enough to fully explain what she had seen on the beach, and, that it was taking a great deal of effort to speak. She let go of trying to communicate. She just let herself think: I am in the kindest and most skillful hands. Let go and heal.

The Magician scooped out a dollop of honey with a small wooden spoon from his little ceramic jar. He then spread it onto the wound. Eva could actually feel it soothe her. Then The Magician turned to the stove in the corner. It was laid, ready for her return. A quick strike of a flint on the hearthstone and it was lit.

Soon warmth came to the small room. The Magician put on some tea, adding some of his dried mushrooms.

"Mm," he said to himself, "I need some rosemary."

Eva heard him. "Everything is in the cupboard on the other side." She vaguely gestured towards a small pine cabinet on the floor beside the head of her bed.

The Magician opened it. There, in little sacks and neatly placed, were a selection of herbs and spices. "Oh, have you been to the King's market?"

"Yes, but unannounced and illusive. Things aren't

good are they?"

"No, though they have turned a corner. But we are getting you better, not discussing affairs of state". The Magician kept rummaging through the little cupboard. "Ah, excellent: rosemary and lemon verbena to go with my sage. Good for both drinking and bathing." He started to hum as he put the herbs in both the tea kettle and a small pot, bringing both to a boil.

The Magician proceeded to potter around the retreat for most of the afternoon, making Eva drink often and bathing the wound with various combinations of herbal tea. Eva was not interested in food, but he did manage to get her to drink some goat's milk and honey.

"Best to let the fever pass before eating too much. I shall leave some milk in your cold store unless, that is, I can convince you to come down and be looked after by us. Lola is excelling herself at domestic duties after her training with Milly."

"My place is here Ellery."

Eva smiled, looking slightly better, but still very weak. The tea was ridding her of the infection, but her body had been seriously weakened by having to exert so much energy whilst injured.

"Very well, but I shall send Lola up with soup tomorrow morning."

"Is that wise? We agreed to wait -"

"Lola has changed," The Magician interrupted. "She has become a young woman overnight. I think she is ready to take on the challenge of meeting you."

The Magician then explained that it was Lola who

had reversed the enchantment of the serpents in the Forest Queen's well. She could now communicate with animals of all kinds and understood the importance of the four directions, which she showed when pacifying the serpents at the well. She now bore the emblem of the King, as did, of course, The Magician and Eva.

Eva listened, moved by his admiration and pride in Lola's achievements. "I have watched her these past years. She is a child of the forest, her mother's daughter. You will have to lift the disguise when you pass the holly-oak tree. I am too weak."

"I will. Is the fox able to keep watch for the night?" asked The Magician.

"Of course. Besides, I can make things seem scary until sunrise. I have the energy for that," Eva replied.

"Very well, I'll be back the day after tomorrow. We'll talk more and figure out who this beach-dweller with a bow and arrow is."

The Magician smiled and started for the door. Isis and Benu took up their positions on the bed and smiled at The Magician with their eyes as he left.

Tara was sitting by the holly-oak tree as The Magician approached the path. *"Guard well my little friend,"* he sent to her and waved his hand.

What had been a series of cliffs and a tangle of trees to any passerby now appeared as a neat set of three caves, half natural and half human-made, built into the side of the mountain.

Tara sat, ready to give warning until sunrise.

The Magician was true to his word and arrived back

at the cottage just as the sun had disappeared behind the ridge. Lola was stirring the soup, supervised by Pixey and Leo. Nanny, Lola's goat, had been milked, the floor swept, and the fires lit. Bread was cut and ready on the table for the evening meal.

"Ah Lola, you have timed things well, and I am a hungry man." The Magician put down his bag and rinsed his hands in a small bowl by the sink which always had a cup of sage tea added to it to fully cleanse their hands before they ate.

"Where have you been? Collecting herbs?" Lola was setting out bowls of the steaming soup.

"No, no, I was seeing a friend. One who is ill. She needs care over the next week or so, I'd like you to help me."

"She?" Lola almost jested.

"It is nothing you might imagine like that, young lady," The Magician said, lightly scolding her. "Eva was my apprentice once, as have been a number of others. She is the closest to me and will take my place when I am no longer here."

Lola was stunned. "Oh, I didn't think…" suddenly her future was in complete disarray. She had imagined, when she came to stay with The Magician, that it would be she who took over from him one day. There would be caring for him when he was very old and eventually living on her own, with all of the animals around her. Except, of course, when the King or his heir requested her presence.

The Magician saw the shock in Lola's face. "You

must have known that, during my very long life, there were other apprentices before you. Indeed, part of the life of the gifted is to pass on their gifts. Perhaps the only thing that is important for the gifted is to pass on their gifts. You will have to do this too one day, my dear."

Lola tried to smile.

"Eva will be very important to you too. Time spent with her is to be part of your training, which is why I think you are ready to meet her now."

Lola was gently blowing on her spoon and looking down at her soup. She took a deep breath. "How will she be important to me?" she asked.

"She will pass on to you things that I cannot. She has similar talents to you and can communicate with the natural world in a way that I cannot. You may need to spend some time up on the mountainside with her this winter."

"Where up on the mountainside?" Lola asked. "I have wandered up there for the last two years and have never seen where she lives."

"Her caves are set on the lower ridge. She has been there all the time, only there has been an enchantment on that ridge. She has been watching you. Have you seen a family of foxes in a set of crumbling cliffs?"

"Yes, I watch them often; they are always the same ones. Sometimes they come very close and almost let me touch their noses."

The Magician chuckled. "That would be Benu and Isis. Only one of them is actually a fox. The other three are Eva and her two cats. Good, then you know exactly where to bring some soup and other provisions tomorrow. Be sure she eats and her fires are well stoked. Oh, and she probably hasn't been up to brushing Benu, who would welcome your attention. No doubt he will be able to tell you where his brush is. He relishes his daily groom."

CHAPTER 2

Connections

Lola rose early the next morning. There had been a thick frost, as it was not many weeks before the longest night, or 'sun-return' as it was called in the Three Valleys. The leaves that covered the ground looked as if they had been trapped inside clusters of crystals, showing off their colour one last time before they disappeared into the earth, feeding it for the following year.

Lola trudged up the path behind the cottage. She carried the largest ceramic flask they had, filled with pumpkin and carrot soup, in one arm and a satchel with cheese, bread and a smaller flask of goat's milk slung over her opposite shoulder. She knew exactly where to go. So many times she had just sat and watched the delightful fox family, never questioning why the smaller foxes hadn't grown up. They had in turn watched her, and contemplated how she had changed over the months and was now turning into a young woman.

As she approached the holly-oak she saw a flash of something orange scuttle up the path before her. Lola proceeded up the path and, as she turned the bend, she saw the neat system of caves that had carefully built stone fronts constructed around them. There were three. One was smaller than the other two and furthest from the edge of the path. There was a fire circle laid out on the ground in front of this little cave. The other two were more like the width of the rooms in The Magician's cottage, but there was no clue as to how deep they went into the mountain. The two larger ones also had awnings constructed of strips of bark and sapling wood. The fox sat under one of these, in front of a door.

"*She's here,*" Lola heard a quiet voice send.

She walked up to ledge. The fox backed away slightly.

"*Thank you,*" Lola sent back.

The fox smiled at her with its eyes.

Lola slowly opened the door. A little light came through one of the windows. The room had a large and high platform bed under which there were pine storage drawers. There was a pine cabinet to one side of the bed and a little cast iron stove in the corner near the window further away from the foot of the bed. In the bed there were the three other 'foxes'. Lola could now clearly see they were two large fluffy cats and a woman.

The woman lay dozing. She was handsome with strong, slightly rounded features. Her hair was dark and cut short, shorter than even a knight's hair, but falling attractively around her face. Her eyebrows were dark and her lips gracefully formed, not smiling, not frowning. Her face told of a life of peace and solitude.

Yet Lola felt unease. There was something too familiar about this woman, even though she had never seen her before.

The woman stirred. Her eyes gently opened and her lips hinted a smile. "Lola," Eva quietly said, "you have come to see me. At last you know that I am here." Eva struggled slightly to sit up, but managed to. She looked pale, though not sickly, her healthy state of being seemed only temporarily interrupted, but soon to return.

"I have brought you some soup." Lola still stood in the same spot with all of her wears. Something about this woman was unnerving her and she didn't quite know what to do or how to act.

"Oh, so you too are learning the great teaching of soup, one that will travel through the ages and nourish all those who hear it. I am Eva, Lola. What has The Magician told you about me?"

"Um, not too much." Lola felt huge waves of emotion creeping into her. This woman, Eva, was too strange yet also too familiar. The feelings made Lola almost dizzy. Then tears started to fill her eyes; her thoughts were of something cruel, too cruel to have actually happened. Her legs started to feel weak under the weight of the flask and satchel. She gently lowered them to the ground without taking her eyes off of Eva.

"What troubles you Lola?" Eva asked, registering the turmoil in Lola's face.

"Are you my mother?" Lola's voice trembled as she spoke.

There was now a silence between them as they looked at each other. A silence that for Lola seemed to last an age.

"No, Lola. Would that I was," Eva now looked at Lola with both tears and a smile. "I am your aunt, Lola, your mother's younger sister."

"Oh," Lola barely said. She didn't know whether she was disappointed or relieved.

"I saw you when you were very small, just days old. I held you and could have taken you for my own, but I was only just finishing my training. I needed to go into retreat for a number of years to complete it, so I let you go. You were not too badly treated by your father's family, I believe." Eva put her hand gently to Lola's face. "You look like them, sun freckled and strawberry blonde and those twinkling blue eyes."

Lola moved closer to Eva and kept her gaze on her. She gently reached over Eva's body and put her hand on the injured arm in sympathy to the wound. Eva smelled of herbs and fresh linen. Lola remembered that smell from the first moments of her own life.

Eva pulled Lola close to her with her good arm. Inside, both felt as if a waterfall gushed between them, washing away a wall - one that had, until now, served them well in following their lonely paths. In their meeting, though, the wall was now gone.

Lola sobbed. Eva too had tears streaming down her face. "It's alright, little one. You are still my little one. Though, oh so brave, I have heard."

"I... I have always felt so alone, needing animals

around me. But I never thought to use the word." Lola continued to sob.

"You were never alone, my dear." Eva pulled away, enough to be able to dry Lola's tears with the sleeve of her night shift.

In all her life Lola couldn't remember anyone doing this. Not even Milly, who would, of course, have done it if Lola had cried in front of her. But she had never cried like this in front of anyone.

"Come sit on the bed." Eva moved over.

Benu and Isis were now sniffing and scenting Lola by rubbing up again her. They could smell Pixey and approved. Lola pulled off her boots and curled up with the three of them.

"We have watched each other for many hours, haven't we?" said Eva. "I have enjoyed every minute of it."

"Me too." Lola's voice was beginning to settle down. "But I am glad one of you really is a fox because I really like foxes. I have a friend who is a fox who helped to save the whole kingdom. She looks after two men who are like my big brothers, more than my real big brothers on the farm, who never thought I could do much. I just couldn't do much that was useful to them, but I can do things, you know."

"Oh, of course you can. Lola, you can do more than you can possibly imagine and we shall do things together for the rest of our lives. Your father is a good man and he loved your mother with all of his heart. He wanted you too, but he knew he would always lose you to me. You have inherited your grandmother's gifts, and probably have some of your own."

"Who was my grandmother?" Lola felt curious and slightly annoyed at the same time. Why had no one mentioned any of this to her before?

"Well," replied Eva, "she was not unlike me, but she had a family first, your mother and I. She mostly delivered babies and all were well. Even when they at first seemed lifeless, she could breathe life into them. She died, though, before you were born. I'm sure your mother would have survived if she had been there to help."

Eva looked kindly at Lola, but Lola could sense unease.

Eva continued. "There is another connection, one I don't think your father is quite clear about. The Magician is your grandmother's brother. He was born ten years after your grandmother."

There was another silence between Lola and Eva now. Lola felt a numb space in her chest, which then was filled with a shaking heat. "Why didn't anybody tell me?" Lola jumped off the bed and threw a scowling look at Eva.

"Because it was more likely you would go deeper into your own resources and pull up your power from your own depths if you didn't know. Children who know they may have inherited power rarely reach their potential. I'm sorry if it feels cruel."

Lola dropped onto a low stool by the fire. "Well, at least I know a little about what I can do myself," she said, quietly putting her face in her hands. Her head was swimming with all kinds of questions and her heart felt as if it had tossed about like a rubber ball.

Eva sat up. She accidentally put too much weight on her injured arm and winced.

Lola looked up. She gave Eva a half smile. "Soup?" she said, feeling embarrassed by her outburst and looking down at the large flask. "It cures everything."

"Yes, perhaps that is a good place to start," said Eva.

Lola helped Eva bathe her wound, tidy the caves and wash out her blood-stained clothes. Eva knew that she still had a fever, but not one that was life threatening, as it had been the day before. She ate soup and continued to drink the tea that The Magician had made.

Wrapped up warmly with her fur boots on, Eva gave Lola a tour of her caves. The middle one was actually the kitchen, though Eva sometimes would heat things up on the little stove in her sleeping cave. In the kitchen was a bigger stove with pots hanging over the top and around the sides on hooks. Herbs of many descriptions hung from the ceiling. It was similar to the way The Magician hung herbs in their cottage. There was also a small round table. A woven cloth of greens and reds covered it. Three chairs stood around the table, also made from pine. They were carefully sanded and waxed to give them a slight shine.

The cave that most interested Lola, though, was the third cave. It was hardly six feet square and had a small fireplace fashioned into one side. Upon the mantle-piece were carvings of forest creatures. Lola could feel both peace and elation when she entered the cave, as if her heart had immediately lightened. Above the mantle-piece was a beautiful tapestry of tall rocky cliffs surrounding a deserted sandy beach. There was a rainbow reaching down into the foreground and a pine forest expanding up the right side of it. Lola felt she could have fallen into the tapestry, as if it was another world, just waiting for her. "Where is that?" she asked.

"My birth place, and your mother's. It is the sea at the end of this valley."

There was another carving on the mantle-piece that did not make Lola so comfortable. It had a body that curved and swirled into a fierce head with horns and menacing fangs. It also had wings. Lola stared at it, feeling frozen and wondering if the call of the serpents could reach this far.

Eva noticed Lola's trepidation. "It is a dragon, Lola, and not to be feared. It is a creature of all the elements, and very important."

"It looks like the serpents that tried to steal our language."

"No, dragons are the makers of language and wisdom, Lola. They're very different to the serpents, who have their own place - but not the place of the dragon," Eva reassured her.

"What do you use this room for?" asked Lola as she shook herself out of the alarm she was feeling.

"Contemplation, meditation, ritual," Eva answered.

"What are they?"

"How you deepen and strengthen your power. I expect you see Ellery, I mean The Magician, do it often, but you may think he is sleeping."

"Well, he does doze in front of the fire a lot, but he doesn't have a room like this, and no dragons."

"Have you been in his room, Lola?" asked Eva.

"No, no I haven't. You called him a name."

"Yes, his name. He was, of course, my Uncle Ellery before he was The Magician. He told me to call him that again once I finished my training."

Lola looked around the room again carefully. There was something about it. Something was in this room that she deeply knew about herself, yet had not yet recognised. Was it that Eva was her aunt? The room seemed to be so much more than just the things in it.

"How long do you spend in this room?" Lola asked.

"A few hours a day perhaps. Much of what I do in my daily life is just an extension of what happens in this room," Eva replied.

"Happens? Do all these things come alive or something? What actually happens?"

Eva smiled. "What actually 'happens', happens within me. Our inner worlds are sometimes more lively than our outer ones. This room is simply a place where we can leave the outer world behind and let the inner world speak. That is often where our deepest wisdom is found. You must have some understanding of that now. No one told you outright how to subdue the serpents."

"Subdue. I don't like that word. The Magician

was telling me about those kinds of words; subdue, transform, conquer. I think I would have preferred to have conquered the serpents. That means getting rid of them for good, doesn't it?"

"Yes, but rarely does conquering mean we are free from conflict. I am glad The Magician is talking to you about these words. Perhaps the Forest Queen tried to conquer them in the end after so many years of subduing them. I don't believe she would have ever willingly let them take her over. She was a wise and beautiful woman." Eva was silent for a moment. "To transform anything we find in our lives, or ourselves, that is out of harmony with our values, we must first understand it, and then transform it if that is possible. Occasionally we just need to accept it."

Lola looked around the room again. Her head hurt. Eva led a very simple life; Lola could see this by the surroundings. But my goodness, thought Lola, did Eva think. Maybe that was why she lived so simply, to make space for all of that thinking.

Eva kindly led Lola towards the door. The sun was now reddening as it leaned towards the west. Both looked towards the western sky.

"You have about an hour before darkness." Eva had her hand on Lola's shoulder to gently steady herself.

"I don't mind walking in the dark," Lola said dreamily, fixated on the changing sky.

"Stoke up the fire and then you must go. I should take some rest."

The two slowly made their way back to the first

cave. Lola stoked up the fire. Benu and Isis stretched out before it on the end of the bed. They would be ready to hunt soon.

"Shall I come again tomorrow?" Lola asked as she put the empty flask into her satchel.

"Come the next day. I am healing well. The fox will come to you if I need you before then."

Lola hesitated and then leaned over and gently kissed Eva on the cheek. "I will bring more soup." Lola backed out the door, carefully closing it, not wanting to take her eyes off Eva.

"I will see you down the cliffs," a small voice sent.

There was Tara, the fox sitting at the top of the path. Lola smiled. She loved seeing foxes, and she was glad that this one was real.

CHAPTER THREE

Castaways

Morgan didn't mind hardship. She had travelled many miles over both land and sea with her father and had coped very well. She hunted, fished and could find her way without a compass; knew how moss and lichen appeared on rocks and trees, and how the sun travelled across the sky to tell the time of day. She did not, however, necessarily like the company of her new mistress, or having a mistress at all.

Morgan had been brought up by her father, a hunter and a woodsman. In the land that they came from he was very much sought after by noble families to keep their estates managed. His preference would be to live alone in the woods, but he wanted Morgan to have choices, so he kept close to society. Morgan had grown to be tall, strong and beautiful. The noble family that he worked for had a daughter a few years younger than her. The Lord offered Morgan the role of companion to his daughter Ariella, having been impressed by the graciousness and intelligence of Morgan's father.

So, Morgan now had the responsibility of Ariella, and things had gone too far.

Morgan sat on the beach with her carving knife,

her sun-burnt hands whittling away at a thin piece of wood for an arrow. The sun picked up the auburn highlights in her straight dark hair. Much slighter than her, Ariella, olive-skinned and darkened by the sun, looked on.

"I'm sure it came down, someone must have taken it. A seagull couldn't break an arrow like that," Ariella said, as she watched Morgan.

"It was our last arrow. Next time let me shoot. It's cruel to injure an animal. Goodness knows where it went to die, and seagulls are not very appetising. Not a bit like chicken. I've tried them."

"Hmm," Ariella sighed. "Still, isn't this better than sitting around father's drawing room learning to be ladies? Waiting for an adventurous suitor to come and tell us his stories? At least this way we have our own stories."

Ariella had convinced Morgan to take her sailing, something she was only a novice at herself, without her father there. Morgan had given into the idea because she was, in fact, as bored with the Lord's drawing room as Ariella.

"Perhaps we should have gone horse riding; horses know their way home." Morgan continued to sharpen the wood for her arrow.

"Oh Morgan, I don't ever want to go home. I suppose I might miss my father eventually, but I do not want the life he has planned for me. I wish I had your father. Your life has been filled with wonder and adventure, mine with antiques and lace. Both are fine occasionally, but one could hardly find meaning in antiques and lace. Just these few last days, watching the sun rise and set, sleeping in our sail tent, they've been the happiest days of my life."

Morgan smiled. Ariella did have a passionate heart that you had to admire, and a short memory. It was only a few hours earlier that she had been complaining of being cold and hungry. Morgan gently pressed the point of the arrow onto her finger.

"Ouch," Morgan jerked her hand away. "That will do. Now, as wondrous as you find this deserted beach, during this time of year it has very little sustenance and we are going to have to start walking. I have been watching the hills. There must be a farm or a village seven or eight miles up that valley. There are thin wisps of smoke which I don't think are mist. They travel further before dispersing. If we travel light, we should be there by nightfall."

"But we were in the boat a day and a night. We have no idea what kind of people might be there. They might capture us, or worse."

Ariella had been brought up to be on her guard against anyone different to herself. It was her father's way of dealing with the world. Always be on the defensive, and never give anyone the benefit of the doubt, unless there was an obvious reward for you.

Morgan's father had a very different philosophy. He taught her to always look for common ground with those she didn't know before she made any kind of a judgment. It had been a philosophy that had served him well and enabled him to provide generously for her.

"I doubt we have anything to worry about, Ariella. If I'm correct in my navigation, we are in The Three Valleys. It's a peaceful, if not very private land. People live here simply, just with nature. Even the King's palace is said to be rustic, though comfortable."

"Well, what if you're wrong? What if there are savages who might want to hold me for ransom? I must disguise myself so there is no hint of the money I have."

Morgan burst out laughing at Ariella's comment. She had to hold her sides and sit down on a rock to steady herself. "You look terrible, there is…" Morgan had to take a breath, "there is absolutely no need for a disguise."

Ariella looked alarmed and felt her hair, stroked her face and looked down at her tattered clothing. Then she smiled. "Of course, well, I imagine you look sort of how you always look, being an outdoors person. I forgot I might look like an outdoors person too."

"Yes, well, think a little more maybe." Morgan was still chuckling as she wound her own long hair into a plait and pushed a small stick through it to keep it up. "Here." She handed Ariella her small wooden comb. "Do the same with your hair while I pack up what I can of our things and wash your face in that rock pool or you'll scare the locals."

Ariella obeyed. She also tried to arrange the tunic, which she had 'borrowed' from the gardening shed, more neatly. She looked up at the valley they were about to walk into and the high mountains beyond. They were covered with trees, unlike her very arid home. She looked down at her rather inadequate boots, which were really not meant for walking, just for show in hunts and outdoor events. "I must be positive, I must be rigorous with myself," she whispered. She tried pulling the comb through the tangled mess of her hair. She immediately turned to Morgan, who was busy sorting out what was left of the small wooden sailing boat and their belongings, to help her. "No, I must do this myself." Ariella began to pull the small comb though the ends of her hair.

After about ten minutes, Ariella had managed to rid herself of most of the tangles in her mass of wavy black hair. Morgan had fashioned two shoulder bags with sail cloth to carry the few warm clothes they had brought and what was left of a small loaf of rustic bread. They also had a few feeble and bruised apples. They had eaten very little for the last two days.

"This one is yours to carry." Morgan draped one of the bags over Ariella's shoulder. "Sling it across yourself, you may need both hands."

"But-" Ariella stopped. "I must do this myself," she said quietly under her breath. She re-determined herself.

"We'll follow the stream, the water is fresh." Morgan leaned down and cupped her hand to take a drink. "Be glad we don't have to carry water."

Ariella looked around. She really had loved the

little corner of this deserted beach, her first experience of freedom ever in her life, but now they were leaving. She wound her hair back and caught it with the strap of her bag. She looked ahead. Morgan was already a hundred yards beyond her and still walking.

"Right, another new thing." Ariella turned her back to the sea and followed.

CHAPTER 4

Soup and Silence

Lola swept and organised the cottage for The Magician all day. Pixey followed her, a bit concerned that Lola seemed so preoccupied. Lola was giving her little attention and not even chatting. Lola would always chat in a human voice as she went through her day, even though she knew Pixey wouldn't understand much of it.

The Magician brought in squashes and other root vegetables from the garden at midday. "We need a rather special soup, Lola," he said as he started to clean and prepare the vegetables. "Do you know what happens tomorrow?"

"I go back to Eva to check on her," replied Lola as she swept around the fireplace in the sitting area.

"Mmm." The Magician was examining a leek to see if it was suitable for his soup. "Yes, you do go and see Eva, and I will come too. It's a good day for me as I can spend it with both of you. Tomorrow marks thirty days before sun return. Thirty quite sacred days. I usually leave you for much of it, but now that you know of Eva we can be together."

"Will we go into her meditation cave?" asked Lola.

"Yes, I expect we will. It's a time to remember all

those who are no longer here. They are closest to us on this day and they follow us into the dark, into the depths of our hearts and help us to find more of ourselves," explained The Magician.

"Will they appear?"

"Possibly. It is more likely that you will contact a feeling for someone you had a strong relationship with. Some say the dead just wander, but actually you have to invite them."

"How do they follow you into the dark? I mean the dark this time of year." Lola was perplexed but realised that this could actually be her first real lesson in magic.

"They guard your mind. They help you understand your direction in life. These next thirty days are the days of stories, contemplation and retreat. The earth is going to sleep. We must become quieter. It is harmful to those who still rush about; it can actually shorten their lives."

"Who rushes about?" Lola had never seen anyone being very energetic at this time of year, other than those who just kept their farms ticking over until it was time to engage with the growing season again.

"Not the people in our valleys so much. We are quite sensible here. But other lands use this time for huge festivals and merry-making. Of course no one says it can't be a happy time, but it is better if that happens in a quiet way." The Magician was continuing to chop his vegetables as he explained, his chop-chopping adding a rhythm to his words.

"Oh." Lola nodded her head. Pixey, who had been

listening, twitched her whiskers. The Magician had talked beyond Lola's understanding again. Lola would have to think about this and just see what the time with Eva and The Magician brought.

Pixey jumped down and started rubbing around Lola and The Magician's legs. *"Can I come?"* she sent. The only part she understood was that Lola was to go out for the day again. *"I don't want to be on my own."*

" Not this time, little one." The Magician was now able to understand Pixey as well as he could Leo. *"Leo will look after you, and we won't be back late."*

The Magician carried on chopping and peeling. "Put some water on, Lola, so it is ready for the vegetables."

Lola smiled. She looked down at Pixey and sent, *"Of course the time of magic must start with soup."*

The Magician hummed to himself as he carried on cooking. Every once in a while he would utter words in his tune. The words made no sense to Lola, but she had occasionally heard him saying the same words to himself while he was reading or just resting with his eyes closed.

So the day passed. There was bread, fruit and cheese and a light broth for supper, but no offering from the pot of soup, which had a strip of cloth tied over the top of its lid.

"The soup has to mature in its own juices overnight." The Magician winked at Lola as she looked at the secure pot curiously from their supper table.

After midday the next day, The Magician saddled up Coal. Lola had wanted to leave first thing, but The

Magician was very clear that Eva would want the early hours of the morning to herself and then time to rest.

Lola fussed over Pixey, promising her that she could come when she was just a little older and when the other cats had been pre-warned. Pixey was still very small, being barely four months old. Lola did agree with The Magician that she was best kept in the care of Leo who had, in Lola's opinion, become the perfect uncle to Pixey.

The Magician was fixing the saddle on Coal and using blankets to make the sitting space smaller.

"I don't mind walking," said Lola as she watched his efforts.

"That's just as well. I'm not arranging this for you, but for the soup."

"The soup," thought Lola, "never has he made such a fuss about the soup."

They were soon on their way, Coal trying very hard to walk gracefully. The Magician had briefed him on the importance of his cargo and, though it was well secured, there was a chance that a little could seep out if Coal was not steady on his feet.

Lola could feel a sense of excitement welling up in her as they climbed. It was a feeling of coming to a place she had always belonged to. It was not an actual place, but a place inside herself. A feeling that she was doing exactly what she was meant to do. All of her worries and questions about life were minimized because she was in the present moment doing what was absolutely necessary.

When they reached the holy-oak the fox stepped out, smiled with her eyes and then scurried up the path.

"*The welcoming committee I think,*" sent Coal who was doing a wonderful job balancing the soup on his back.

"*We can take it from here, old friend.*" The Magician went over to Coal and began to unwrap the soup. He handed the pot to Lola. "Hold this carefully, I'll take it back in a moment". He then loosened Coal's saddle but left the blanket on. He carefully led Coal to a small break in the trees with a grassy area and a stream running by it. "*Hopefully, you will be comfortable here for the day.*" He stroked Coal's mane and gave him a pat on the neck.

The Magician returned to Lola and took the pot. They both carried on up the rocky slope. They carefully negotiated the path, one that Coal would have found very difficult. To Lola it had a familiar feel that she now understood, and her joy of the day continued.

As they rounded the bend, Eva appeared on the ledge. She was much changed. Her short hair was now clean and brushed so it fell softly around her face with a gentle wave in the fringe. The colour in her handsome face had returned to being both rosy and tanned. She had light hazel eyes that were set off by her dark eyebrows.

"You have brought the soup," she said, smiling as she started coming down the path to meet them.

Lola noticed that Eva had boots almost identical

to her own. She wore a deep red tunic with purple embroidery around the standup collar neck. It looked special. Unlike other women, she wore leggings, similar to a man's, but more flattering, being tighter around her legs. She wore simple jewelry, made of small shells and forest offerings. She didn't look masculine, but she was different to other women.

"Have you been to the pool?" The Magician enquired as he handed over the soup to Eva.

"Yes, it was a challenge. I had to go in and swim as myself. I didn't have the energy to change, but the water has done its job and I was probably healed more as a result of not changing."

"You do look better Eva. I'm relieved."

The Magician followed Eva up the hill. Lola followed after, not quite understanding what was being said about the pool, but thinking perhaps that being able to bathe might have helped Eva. She was certainly able to carry the heavy soup pot.

When they reached the ledge they found a well-prepared fire with a tripod, ready and waiting. Lola could tell it was cedar wood being burned, a very sacred wood. Eva carefully took the cloth off the pot and skillfully hung it on the tripod. She then removed the lid and sniffed. "I think you have excelled yourself this time Ellery."

"Well, I had to, having you both together at last." The Magician was making himself at home on a stool by the fire.

Eva looked up, "Lola, there are bowls inside on the

table and a ladle. Would you fetch them?"

Lola, who realised she was standing there without knowing what to do, nodded her head and hurried to the kitchen cave to get the bowls.

Eva looked at The Magician. "Do you think she is ready?"

"We are both here to support her," The Magician reassured Eva.

Benu wandered onto the ledge and started to weave in and out of The Magician's legs just as Lola appeared. "Lola," The Magician beckoned, "come and sit. Have you come to know this fine fellow?"

Lola could feel the slight tension that Eva's question to The Magician had created, but the appearance of Benu put everyone at ease. She handed the ladle to Eva and put the bowls by the fire to warm. Now Isis, not wanting to be left out, appeared from her spot on the veranda and jumped onto Lola's lap. Isis knew what was happening. She had seen through many nights of the dead. Looking after Lola was her responsibility today.

The soup soon started to simmer. Eva stirred it and then looked to The Magician. He raised his eyebrows in consent. "It should be ready, my dear. It simmered most of the night."

Eva smiled. She had eaten gallons of the Magician's soup and she was quite sure it was what made her so robust. Yet she could never quite match his skill. His soup was the one teaching that she hadn't yet mastered.

Eva carefully ladled out the soup to Lola and The Magician, and then to herself.

"Careful not to leave a drop, Lola." The Magician winked. "We've a big night ahead."

Isis had laid herself flat on Lola's lap to make room for Lola to eat, but had no intention of leaving. *"I shall be your guardian in practice until we can get that kitten of yours trained."* Isis seemed to purr through her sending.

"My guardian? What do you mean?" Lola sent back, while carefully sipping her soup from her little ladle.

"You'll see, you mustn't worry. You will be safe with me."

Eva glanced over at Isis with a slight cautioning look. Isis smirked with her eyes and then, still stretched out, started cleaning her toes on her front paws.

"What Isis is trying to tell you, Lola, is that when we practice we go into the realms of our minds and this connects us with those outside of our world, especially on this night. We need to stay grounded though, in this world. So, we have a guardian. An animal is best, one that understands the process, because they are so bound to this earth. Isis is a good guardian for you. Though Pixey will learn, she is far too young yet. Benu can be with me and The Magician can have Tara."

"Tara?" Lola looked about for another cat.

"The fox," said The Magician. "One of my favourite creatures you know."

Lola noticed the soup had a special flavour. The Magician must have put in a different set of herbs than he usually did. It was refreshing and filling. Lola soon started to feel energized, yet, very peaceful and very present.

As Lola finished her bowl, Eva smiled and took it from her. "I'll rinse these in the stream. You and The Magician must go along the path and find offerings for the practice cave."

"Offerings?" Lola asked.

"Come, I will show you Lola. You cannot invite the dead without asking the living spirits to join in."

Lola followed The Magician down the path past the caves. She had never been there before. She hadn't wanted to disturb the 'foxes'.

The path was rocky with a little vegetation along it. The Magician pointed out a number of very precious herbs that only grew near sacred water, which he explained was in a pool at the end of the path.

The herbs they collected looked insignificant, but had a very pungent smell. Lola noticed that The Magician only took very small amounts and mumbled a quiet incantation as he did. "You must always ask permission of nature to take from her."

Lola had heard him say this many times, but now it seemed more significant than ever.

They had been slowly meandering along for about half an hour when they turned a bend in the path. There in front of them was a deep, green pool of water, surrounded on three sides by silver-grey stone cliffs. A waterfall gracefully tumbled over the top of the cliff. Lola stopped, spell bound by the scene. She found herself fascinated by the gentle lapping of the ripples as they came up to the small strip of sand that edged the side of the pool where she stood.

"Is this the sacred water?" she whispered to The Magician.

"Yes. A gateway to another world. One that you will one day be able to pass through to."

"Me?" Lola more mouthed than whispered.

"Yes, Lola, you. You were always meant to be one of the ones who could pass between this world and another. Yes," The Magician said again, quietly to himself. "Come, rinse your hands and face. You will feel refreshed and can introduce yourself to it at the same time. The sacred water takes a while to get to know you."

The Magician knelt down. Elegantly, he spread his large gnarled hands over the water and gently lowered them to the surface. He then cupped them around until his palms faced up. Lifting a small amount of water to his face, he reverently wet his beard and temple. He was then still, eyes closed, breath held for a moment. Finally breathing out with a satisfied sigh, he looked at Lola who had been watching his every move.

"Go on, it's lovely," he whispered.

Lola tried very hard to repeat The Magician's ritual. As she put her hands, palms down, over the surface of the water she could feel a quiver coming from below, as if energy was gently bubbling up to meet her. She looked at The Magician in alarm.

"It's alright, it's just coming up to say hello," he reassured her.

Lola continued trying to do everything she had seen The Magician do. She was as gentle and reverent with the water as he had been. When she finally lifted the water to her face, it was cold and made her skin tingle, but there was also a feeling of light, as if sunbeams caught in the water were playfully dancing across her cheeks. It was like a tickle deep inside her smile that made her smile even more. She looked up and saw that The Magician was smiling too.

They walked back in silence towards Eva's caves, sometimes stopping to watch a bird or a squirrel, sometimes seeing a few things dropped on the path, like leaves or acorns, which Lola would arrange in a pretty pattern at the roots of trees to show her respect for them. She had never experienced the forest in this much detail. She felt completely insignificant, yet totally connected with everything around her. She could have easily been a stone or a twig and she would have been just as happy.

As they rounded the last bend, there was a rowan tree, still donned with its golden leaves and bursting with rust-red berries. Lola looked at The Magician and then addressed the tree.

"I would like one of your small branches to offer to Eva's shrine. Would it be alright?"

A small bough drooped gracefully onto Lola's shoulder and a sweet melodic voice sang, *"Please take this. It is small and likely to fall off in a storm. Eva's shrine is more fitting than the path underfoot."*

The branch quietly snapped and fell across Lola's shoulder and into her hand. The Magician stood back while this all happened, knowing that Lola had created this moment for herself from her own connection with the woods.

Lola looked at The Magician again and then turned back to the tree. *"Thank you,"* she whispered in her mind. A slight breeze made the tree shudder, almost as if it gave out a little giggle.

They carried on to Eva's caves. The sky was now beginning to glow, ready to give forth a spectacular array of colour as the sun set and continued its journey around the earth.

Eva was waiting when they arrived, dressed in her red flowing tunic with a matching cloak. She held a red and purple shawl over her arm, made of soft wool. It was thin, but warm. The air was starting to feel cold. Eva smiled as she put the shawl around Lola's shoulders.

"Your mother wore this before you were born. I have been saving it for you."

Lola smiled quietly at the gesture, and then holding her rowan branch, continued into the meditation cave, closely followed by Eva and The Magician. Lola took her place on the middle of three sets of cushions where Isis was waiting for her. Benu and Tara were either side. Eva and The Magician took their places respectively and thus the evening began.

Eva had lit many candles around the cave and there was a small fire burning in the fireplace. Both gave off light and warmth. They could have been in a cottage sitting around a fire, cosy and warm. But Lola had a feeling that something more than a friendly chat was going to be asked of her. Isis lovingly draped herself over Lola's lap and prodded the red and purple shawl. But for Isis's purring, they sat in silence.

After what seemed like a long time to Lola, Eva rang a small bell. Isis was quiet now, sitting peacefully, as cats often do, in a semi-meditative state, aware of everything around them.

"We come together to honour our ancestors, our loved ones, who gave us joy in our lives." Eva's voice was melodic and soothing. "We come together to send compassion to those who still have suffering in their souls, may they be free from suffering." Eva rang another bell. "We come together to honour the forest, our friends and teachers in nature." Eva rang another bell. "We come together to welcome the forces of nature, the fusion of the elements - earth, water, fire, air, and mind - to recognise all these within us, and in nature, and to gain knowledge of ourselves from the wisdom the universe has to share." Eva now rang a bell three times. She then started chanting a melodic incantation, one that was soothing, her voice sweet but strong.

Lola, who had been very restless, as she never liked to sit still, felt her energy calm as Eva had started talking. Her legs, which had been stiff and uncomfortable, now felt as if they were melting into the floor. Isis gently adjusted her position and began to purr.

"*Listen to my purr,*" Isis sent to Lola, "*but go where your mind takes you. I shall be here, waiting.*"

Lola relaxed more. Her back-bone seemed to fall

into the cushion and grow upwards at the same time. Her chest expanded and she felt her heart open, as if it was as wide as the universe. Her face tingled and she could feel a gentle smile forming. Lola's breath relaxed her face as it entered her body and travelled down through her heart centre and then back out again.

Somewhere very far away she heard Eva say, "Wherever you go, whom-ever you meet, it is alright. Be open, do not judge, and accept all you see." The kindness in Eva's voice was beyond anything Lola had known kindness could be.

Carefully, but surely, keeping Isis's purring in the back of her mind, Lola let go. She could see a rolling green landscape with grassy hillocks and clumps of wild flowers. There, a woman stood with long, flowing auburn hair, strong, long limbs, a graceful face and a sparkling smile. At first Lola thought she was seeing Eva when Eva was younger, but then she noticed that this woman did not have quite the same look in her eyes. The woman's eyes were brown, her nose a bit longer, and her eyebrows a bit thinner. It was Lola's mother. Lola knew this. Although having no idea what her mother actually looked like, she just knew it was her.

"I'm so proud of you Lola. You have grown to be so lovely." The woman picked a buttercup and gently brushed it across Lola's cheek. Lola felt a tingle of warmth as if a little bit of the sun had been caught in the flower and was leaving a hint of the light behind.

Lola's heart centre welled up and seemed to open.

She could still hear Isis purring. Lola watched her mother's face, searching her eyes for any knowledge that her mother might pass on.

But then the image began to change. Her mother's straight, auburn hair became dark and wavy, her face slightly smaller and paler. The eyes became green and were sadder as her facial features changed and shifted. The bright open background was now darkness and the face before Lola was that of the Forest Queen.

"Lola, I have much to teach you, come back to me."

There was no longer the harsh tone in the Forest Queen's voice that Lola remembered. Instead it was soft and pleading, with an almost loving tone. Then the scene became darker, except for a glowing ring of what looked like flames. The Forest Queen's expression became more distressed and then slowly faded. In her place was movement, slithering movement and a low hiss. This time there was no language, just thought. *"We wait for you Lola. We need you here."*

The serpents' faces emerged out of the ring of glowing flames. At first they looked passive, then they were on the attack, then passive again. Lola could not tell whether the message was entreating her or threatening her. But she remembered what Eva had said: be open to whatever happens.

Isis began to purr loudly now. She knew Lola had gone to another place. She had gone very far for the first time, perhaps further than she should. Isis gently lifted her paw and brushed Lola's cheek. *"Come back Lola, there is always another time, come back now."*

Lola could feel Isis pulling her back, away from the serpents. She felt fear and longing for them at the same time, but Isis was right; she had gone far enough. Reluctantly, she started to withdraw her mind from the serpents. It felt like pulling backwards through a long blue-black tunnel made of nothing. Lola began to feel her arms and legs again. She shuddered and pulled her legs up from their crossed position and hugged them. Isis jumped and landed in front of her. The purring continued and Isis circled around Lola, rubbing up against her and scenting her with the side of her face.

Lola opened her eyes. She looked around. The others were completely still. Both had their animals sitting, eyes closed, on their laps. Tara's whiskers twitched in the air as Isis walked past. The candles had burned down considerably and the fire was just embers. Lola was feeling a chill. She wrapped her mother's shawl around herself tightly and nestled down on her cushions.

"*Well done, Lola,*" Isis sent. "*Sleep now. The others will look after you when they finish.*"

Lola nestled down, putting her head on the cushions. Isis placed her body along Lola's spine to keep her back as warm as possible. "*Sleep now,*" Isis sent again in a whisper.

CHAPTER 5

A Wisp of Smoke

Lola woke to the sound of purring. But it wasn't Isis, it was Pixey's purring. Lola knew this sound better than most anything, as Pixey would purr at the slightest cause. Lola was still wrapped in the red and purple shawl, but another blanket, the soft gray one from her bed had been wrapped around her too, and tucked over her feet to keep them warm.

Lola tried to focus on her surroundings. There was a dim light across the room, but it confused her. She was not used to looking at this particular room from this particular angle. Lola looked down at her arms. They were resting in a comfortable chair, The Magician's chair, while her feet had been propped up on his small stool. She looked over at her own chair and Leo was sat there, his chair empty but for the small blanket she had knitted him with an 'L' on it.

Lola shyly smiled at Leo and he smiled back with his eyes. *"I think you are too big for him to carry up your ladder."* Now Lola began to understand. The Magician must have put her in his chair. Yet, she remembered nothing after curling up and falling asleep in the meditation cave.

"Did he carry me back?" she asked Leo.

"No, the horse. He came back very late with the horse."

"It was so late I fell asleep. I was trying to stay awake, but you were so long. I don't like you being away so long," Pixey sent as she started trying to roll about on Lola's lap and play with the edges of the shawl. She couldn't help herself; everything in life seemed to be a potential plaything. Leo would remind her that one day she would have to be serious, but she didn't look forward to that day.

"You are Lola's familiar," Leo sent, feeling the need to lecture grow as she became distracted by her game. *"You have the responsibility of looking after her."*

"I watch everything she does and help her to do things." Pixey continued the game of catching the corners of the shawl.

"You are good at looking after me, and you will learn even more when you are bigger. You are barely four months old, not big enough to have too much responsibility other than making me laugh," sent Lola.

Lola giggled at Pixey as she kept rolling back and forth. She was warm wrapped in her blanket and felt content just to sit there in the company of Pixey and Leo and watch the sun rise. She thought about meeting her mother, the Forest Queen and the serpents. It felt like a lifetime ago. Her mother was beautiful and the Forest Queen was beautiful too, but so sad. And the serpents, well, they confused her. She couldn't tell whether they were still evil.

Usually, she would have gone running to The Magician and bombarded him with questions, but now, just for now, she wanted to sit quietly and reflect.

Later that day, after much dozing in the Magician's chair and frequent cups of tea with warm bread, Lola got up properly and washed, milked Nanny and started pottering about the cottage. She tidied a little, dusted a little, swept a little, and all the while Pixey followed her, observing very carefully. Pixey sensed a new seriousness in Lola, one that she had to learn about.

Lola didn't talk to Pixey about what had happened, but Pixey picked up little bits of what was going through Lola's mind. Pixey decided she wasn't at all keen on the serpent part of Lola's experience, but she was sure that she and Lola together could sort them out, when she was a bit bigger of course.

The Magician spent the day in much the same way as Lola: brewing tea, reading when he finally got his chair back, straightening his books. Finally, in the evening, they sat with soup, cheese and bread before them. Neither was very hungry, but they had arrived at that part of the day called supper, where the afternoon is turned into evening and the fires are stoked up to last until bedtime.

The Magician looked at Lola and smiled somewhat shyly. "Do you have any questions about last night?" he asked.

Lola met his eyes, nearly smiled and then looked down, trying to think very carefully. Then she looked up again. "I'm sure I will, but not yet. I can't think what to ask yet."

The Magician's quiet smile turned into a broad

grin. "Well done Lola, you have done yourself proud. You have learned about giving yourself time to reflect."

They ate in silence, peaceful comfortable silence.

* * * * * * * *

Morgan turned slightly under the salt-drenched cloak. Half of her was warmish, the other half freezing and sore. She imagined Ariella was the same. They had managed to climb about eight miles up a rocky ravine, but darkness fell so quickly because of the sheer rock walls either side of the path that they had had to stop for the night. There had been enough wood around to make a fire, but now that had gone out.

"Ariella." Morgan shook her slightly. "Ariella, we need to get moving. The sun is coming up. We need to find food and shelter; we can't stay out in this cold."

"I'm so cold, I can't move," groaned Ariella.

"Yes, well this is part of freedom," Morgan reminded her.

Ariella tried to sit up. She felt dizzy and exhausted. Every part of her seemed both numb and in throbbing pain at the same time. "I just don't know if I can," she whimpered.

Morgan looked at the struggling Ariella. She was flushed, which wasn't good. They had to get some help. She felt Ariella's head, it was hot, and her hands were cold, very cold.

"If you don't, you will die. We *must* go." Morgan took Ariella by the arm, part in anger, part in frustration and part in genuine concern. She pulled her roughly to her feet.

"You have to stand; you have to walk." Then Morgan stopped. She turned and looked at last night's fire and sniffed. There was no smoke left in it. She turned towards the top of ravine. Yes, a smell, the faint smell of wood smoke was coming from that direction. "Just a little way. As soon as we see a building you can stop and I'll get some help, but not until then."

Morgan collected what was worth collecting and put it in one bag. This was slung over one shoulder with Ariella supported on her other arm. "Come, one step and then another."

Ariella's head was spinning. She did just what Morgan asked, she had no energy to protest; just one foot, then the next. The path was rocky and steep. Ariella's shoes only just protected her feet from the sharp edges of the shale outcrops. She kept repeating to herself in her head, 'One foot, then the next. Like the stairs at home, I always climb the stairs.'

The two slowly made their way up another hundred feet to the edge of the ravine. There they found a ledge, a grassy ledge, which meant at least the going would be easier. Then elation swelled up in Morgan again with the faint smell of wood smoke growing and the sound of sheep bleating.

"Right, I'm pushing you up over this ledge. Pull yourself on your stomach. I'm right behind you." Morgan wrapped one arm around Ariella's thighs and then pushed her bottom up over the top of the ledge.

She was, at this point, pleased about the delicateness of Ariella's physic as she herself had very little strength left. "Find something to grab onto and pull yourself up."

Again, Ariella had no strength to answer. She just did what Morgan said. As her head rose above the ledge, she could see a field bordered only by a low hedge. She grabbed a small hazel stump and, with all her might, pulled as Morgan pushed. There was rubble and roots that grazed her stomach, but enough space to drag herself up and now she too could smell the wood smoke.

Morgan looked at the ledge she now had to climb. If she asked Ariella to give her a hand down, they might both fall back again. She would just have to use all the energy she had at once to climb it. She focused on the centre of her body and felt her strength there, then using her arms and legs equally, she lunged towards the ledge and scrambled halfway up. As her head cleared the top, Ariella's hand reached out to pull her towards the hazel stump. She dragged herself the rest of the way.

"There, we're up." Ariella's voice sounded laboured, but she was upright and half smiling.

"Wood smoke, can you smell it?" Morgan stood up to survey the surrounding fields. In the dawn light she could see a small wisp of smoke coming out of a small indent in the fields. It was no more than half a mile away, she hoped. Sometimes the dawn could play tricks with distances.

"Come over this hedge and leave our things. We can always come back for them, it's not far." Morgan put all of her effort now into supporting Ariella. They made their way up a large triangular field. There were sheep sheltering on the other side against the hedges. The frosted grass crunched under their feet. 'Lucky sheep with all that wool,' Morgan thought to herself.

Ariella began to cough.

"Come, come on. It's not far, it can't be. I can't leave you out here now." Morgan didn't feel frustration, just pure determination, though the biting cold shuddered through to her bones.   The fight for survival changes your view from one minute to the next, depending on how likely you are to succeed, she thought.

They made their way over another style and found a track between two fields.

"This is good. Can't be far now." Morgan was now panting with every word. She held Ariella upright as she practically dragged her along. Ariella kept coughing.

A dog barked, only yards away around the bend. Then a young man appeared, his collie by his side, barking even more when he saw the girls.

"What the devil?" was all Morgan heard. Then she felt her legs give out from beneath her.

* * * * * * * *

Rory carried Morgan while his wife Stella helped Ariella as best she could along the path.   Ariella continued to cough and shiver, even though Stella had wrapped her warmest woolen shawl around her. Ariella was grateful for the warmth, but had not experienced wool knit quite so rough as this.

"Dear heavens, how did you two come to be so ragged? Goodness, goodness me. Well, never mind. Don't talk now. Let's get you inside and warm." Stella's voice had an air of panic, but also command as if she knew exactly what she would do to get the exhaustion and hunger of the two girls under control. "Boblin!" she called out as they entered the yard. "Boblin, come quick!"

Rory's younger brother appeared from the milking barn holding a rope and a bucket he was using to tie up food to one of the cow stalls. The sight of the two girls made him drop both.

"Caitlin… Caitlin, come. Stella needs help!" He started towards them.

"Never mind us." Stella waived him away. "You get up on one of those horses and go to the retreat. Get one of those healers down here where they are needed, rather than up there where they have only the foxes for their company."

Rory and Stella carried on towards the house. A slightly smaller and younger woman, with sharp features and mousy brown hair, came out of the door. Stella puffed away a strand of her red hair from her freckled face as she helped Ariella towards the young woman.

"Caitlin, we'll put them in our bed." She glanced

back at Rory who quickly nodded. "Boil lots of water. Heat up some of that broth from last night, then thin down some goat's milk and add honey. Goat's milk won't cause so much congestion and has more goodness. Oh, bless us, Nanny," Stella said to the air after she had given her instructions, just hoping it would make a difference.

Rory carried Morgan into a generously sized room for a farmhouse, where there was a double bed covered with a knitted blanket and white linen. The bed was already crisply made although it was hardly past dawn. Stella believed in leaving a trail of order, although her husband's family often left a trail of chaos. She made Caitlin, her brother-in-law's wife and her junior, an ally in fully supporting this cause.

"On top of the blankets," Stella instructed. "They smell of the sea. We'll need to damp bathe them and change their clothes. Caitlin, have you got some clean shifts? They are quite small."

Caitlin appeared. "This might be fitting for the little one. Lola never took it," she said, looking over at the girls. "I'll get a spare one of mine for the other, she's a bit bigger." Though she had a sharp face and a piercing look, Caitlin's voice was soft and full of kindness.

Stella, on the other hand, had much softer looks, yet her voice was the stern one, and she was definitely in charge.

Rory stood at the door, still mesmerised by the presence of the two bedraggled but beautiful young women. "Be off with you, we can manage from here."

Stella shooed him away.

Morgan was aware of the bustle around her, but was so exhausted she could barely respond to anything that was said. She tried to be helpful by turning her elbow or shoulder the right way to get herself out of her salt-drenched clothes, but she was so disorientated that she became confused about which way was on and which way was off.

Ariella, on the other hand, was used to being dressed and undressed by her maids. She had been all her life. So, for this part of the adventure, she was the more successful one. She continued to cough through a warm sponge bath, appreciating the hint of lavender and something lemony over the smell of the farm.

Finally the two girls were settled, warm and clean, with the knitted blanket and crisp sheets pulled up around their chins. Caitlin appeared again as Stella was propping up the pillows behind them. She carried two mugs, one of which she handed to Stella, who took it and made her way around to Morgan's side of the bed. Caitlin stayed with Ariella, whose coughing had subsided a little. Sage, a strong smell of sage and fennel came from the mugs.

"Take as much as you can of this. It will warm you, ease your cough and it's good for the stomach. We'll give you some milk and honey in an hour or so," promised Stella. "There are terrible things that can happen if you eat solids too quickly after you have been starving."

While encouraging her to drink, Caitlin gently

pinched the back of Ariella's slender hand. The loose skin stayed in a peak for nearly ten seconds. "As I thought, completely dehydrated. Drinking is very important," Caitlin said as she encouraged Ariella to take more.

Ariella just looked willingly at Caitlin and sipped as instructed, grateful for the liquid soothing her mouth and throat.

Morgan sipped to the best of her ability. Stella had to spoon in some of the tea. Finally, both girls had drunk a cup. Caitlin took both mugs. Stella sat back in the low wicker chair at the end of the bed, meant for nursing babies.

"I'll sit with them for now while I mend," said Stella as she reached for a wicker basket by the chair. "We'll swap over after some milk and honey later. There's bread rising. It needs to go into the oven in an hour."

Caitlin half smiled at Stella and then looked back at the two girls, both now with their eyes closed. Both had laboured breathing and were pale. She and Stella would bring them through.

CHAPTER 6

A Message Brought

Neither Morgan nor Ariella remembered falling asleep, but sleep they did. The warm goat's milk and honey, alternated with fennel and sage tea every hour, hardly passed their notice compared to the deep senseless sleep they both had. Ariella was propped up to ease her coughing. Morgan curled up like a small child next to her.

It was Ariella who noticed the luring smell of baking bread. It pulled her out of her deep sleep and started to make her stomach churn with excitement. She opened her eyes to see Caitlin sitting in the nursing chair by a well stoked fire. A pile of woolen socks lay at her feet. One sock was in Caitlin's hands while she pushed a needle attached to strong wool through the toe with a gentle rhythm.

"I can smell bread." Ariella couldn't think of anything else to say.

Caitlin looked up and she smiled. When she smiled, the sweetness in her voice shone in her face. "Does it make you hungry?"

Ariella tried to sit up further, thus making Morgan stir. "Yes," said Ariella, "it does make me hungry."

"That is a good sign," replied Caitlin, "but, before

we give you solid food, you must be checked over."

Morgan was now trying to sit up. Caitlin put down her darning and came over to the bed to prop up pillows and secure shawls around the girls' shoulders.

"There will be someone along soon to make sure we are doing the right thing. Then you can have a little bread with your milk and honey," Caitlin reassured them.

A dog barked in the farm-yard. It reminded Morgan of her own dog, Sona. The sound made her realise she missed Sona terribly. Sona was a grey and white collie-like dog. She was perfectly trained and a constant companion, except when Morgan was being Ariella's companion, which was most of the time these days. She had managed to keep Sona to the back of her mind until that moment.

"Sounds like Sona," Morgan said quietly, mostly to herself.

Ariella was not fond of dogs. She flinched at the sound, but knew Morgan must be missing Sona and tried to give her an understanding look.

The bedroom door swung open and Stella whooshed in. "Are we both awake?" She directed this towards Caitlin, who looked over at Morgan and Ariella, guiding Stella's eyes to them. "Ah, good. Yes."

Stella turned and went back out, returning moments later with an old man in a long dark red robe. His beard was neatly trimmed and his hair combed back from his face. His kind eyes had wrinkles around them, indicating that he smiled often.

"Hello ladies," he said, "they call me The Magician, but I'm not sure that is true. How do you both feel?"

Behind The Magician, Lola watched, mesmerised by the two beautiful young women sitting in her brother's bed. She felt quite stirred by being in her old home. Boblin had arrived at midday on his horse. Coal and The Magician had followed her and her brother back down the hill quickly, as they were told the girls were near death.

The Magician kindly took each of their hands, checked them for dehydration, felt their foreheads for fever and examined the colour in their faces. "I think Stella and Caitlin are doing what they should be doing for you," he said. "We can put you on solids tonight, then something with a bit more protein tomorrow. But perhaps you will tell us how you came to be here."

The girls looked at each other. Neither of them knew what to say. Morgan looked down at the knitted blanket on the bed and fiddled with the end of the wool. Ariella looked around at all the people in the room.

"Maybe it's not quite time yet," suggested Caitlin who felt she should champion the girls.

"Mmm," said The Magician, "Is there anyone we should send a message to so that they know you are safe?"

Ariella took a deep breath, "No, no one at the moment."

The dog barked again and Morgan missed Sona even more. "We came by boat. I have no idea how to contact home." Morgan was still looking at the knitted blanket.

"Ah, the shipwreck," said The Magician. Both girls looked up at him startled, wondering how he knew this. The Magician's eyes twinkled. "I think you had an altercation with a seagull I know. But she's better now, not to worry."

Morgan looked at Ariella as if to say, 'I told you so.'

"Well, that's enough for now." He smiled at the girls to try to ease their alarm. "Caitlin and Stella, I've brought some much stronger honey you can mix with balsam for coughs. It will make healing much faster." He then turned towards Lola. "Lola, help Caitlin and Stella make up the medicines and see them through the night. I'll come back in the morning to collect you."

"But what about Pixey and Leo?" whispered Lola. She didn't want to be away another night.

"I'll be sure they are alright," The Magician quietly replied. "Don't worry. I must see Eva and quickly. I'll be back in the morning. You'll learn a lot from Caitlin and Stella. I don't want you in the cottage on your own just in case someone does come looking for them and is not very happy that they are missing."

"Alright," Lola whispered sadly. "You will explain to Pixey that it's just until the morning and make sure the fire is warm for them?"

"Of course." The Magician squeezed Lola's shoulders and was gone. He never did things like that, it surprised Lola, but was mildly comforting all the same.

Magicians have all kinds of skills that they don't

talk about. One of them is fast walking. The Magician could make better progress than he would on Coal. This he would only ever do on his own. He didn't yet want Lola to see him doing this, or know what he was going to ask of Eva.

As he promised, he stopped at the cottage and stoked the fire and made his apologies to Leo and Pixey, promising that he would be back in the next few hours whilst Lola would return in the morning. He then carried on up the hill, fast walking. He only did this in emergencies, but Eva's way of travelling fast was even more efficient if she was well enough.

As he reached the holly-oak, he called out, "Eva!".

Tara was there and quickly scurried up the path to announce the news of his arrival.

Eva appeared on the ledge just outside her sleeping cave, wrapped in her deep red shawl. "Ellery, you are back quickly from the farm." The sun was just beginning to set and there was a faint glow from inside the cave. "Shall I make tea?"

"There is probably no time for that. If you are quite fit, can you change? Can you fly?"

Eva rotated her shoulder. There was a stiffness and a bit of pain, but she knew it was just sore tissue in the muscle that had healed. "I suppose so, if I wasn't too big."

"Good, a small owl will do."

"Where am I to fly?"

"The King, to the Middle Valley. The 'shipwreck' has arrived at the farm and the daughter of a noble warlord from beyond the Eastern Valley is one of the castaways. I would recognise his daughter anywhere. Without the Forest Queen protecting the seas, it may be possible for anyone to get past the boundaries of our kingdom. This warlord does not take lightly to losing things that are valuable to him, especially his daughter."

"How would he know where she went?"

"He wouldn't, but he'll have scouts out to every land within a hundred miles of him and they may not be very reasonable ones. You must let the King know that our valleys need to be properly patrolled. I'm not sure the girls want to be found, so we'll need to handle this very carefully. The other girl is a daughter of a man I once met in these valleys. He had managed to sail through to our shores, a most unusual feat. He is a skilled sailor and woodsman. He went back to his own land to be with his sweetheart, I was told, but never returned. That was more than eighteen years ago. His plan was to return to our valleys and live quietly with her. I sensed him strongly in the girl's mind."

"Will this lord cause trouble if he finds the girls here?"

"I think he will already be causing trouble for the man I spoke of, and he is a very good man. I was disappointed when he never returned. But his skills will be too valuable for the warlord to get rid of him. You see, he could track anything. Hopefully, the lord will see him as too useful a person to throw in a dungeon or worse." The Magician paused and thought.

He couldn't abide power for power's sake. It was why he chose to live how and where he did. "Eva, you know enough, a small owl. She should get you there. Remember Seth's owl. Be sure to keep yourself safe by sending to him when you are close enough."

Eva nodded and raised her arms. Seconds later she was gone, except for the faint cry of a barn owl in the distance.

Flight is a wonderful thing if you don't think too much about how it works. Of course, a barn owl feels completely at ease in the air. Eva loved the sense of flight, but this time it was a bit of a challenge. The air thinned over the pass into the Middle Valley. There were up-drafts and down-drafts that could jostle a small bird around. Eagles, even Ravens, might travel this route with ease, but not at night. The barn owl was the best plan and one of the birds she had mastered. There was a stiffness in her right wing, but it was sturdy none the less. She could, of course, drop down and run as a wolf, but she wasn't sure if all the wolves understood that the Forest Serpents, as Eva liked to think of them, had been tamed. They may sense the human in her and attack.

The night was clear and still, and becoming very frosty. Eva loved these nights. Diamonds appeared on everything as she ventured across the moonlit landscape. The way was steady. There were no unexpected rushes of air to throw her off course.

She was now soaring over the very dark woods below the tree line on the east side. Soon she would see the last lights of the castle glowing. Seth, the owl, and his mate might be patrolling. She called out and sent her presence.

A much deeper and shriller call came back. They had heard her. Then seconds later she saw two enormous wing spans rise above the trees, dark, darker than the sky. They called to her in unison.

"Come, come we will escort you. No one under our protection comes to any harm."

Eva swooped down towards them. They were double her size and mass. As she got closer she felt the air stream they were leaving. She just relaxed and rode, going faster than she would have dared on her own, keeping her wings tilted just so, preventing her from turning into a spin.

"I need to see the King and quickly," she sent. *"Alone, if possible."*

The two owls tilted and then glided towards the top parapet. Seth was on watch. He could feel his owl-self coming towards him. He could feel the thrill of flight. The two owls swooped only inches from the sides of the castle walls and then pulled upwards. Eva was herself again before her feet gently touched the ground, having ridden in on their tail feathers.

"Eva," whispered Seth. He smiled shyly. "You surprise us. Worrying news?"

"Possibly, I need to see the King. I'm afraid this news might keep you rather busy." Eva smiled back. Despite being younger than her, she had always had a soft spot for Seth. She remembered when she had first come to court as The Magician's apprentice. Seth was just finding his feet, learning how to charm the stable hands into a ride around the market or a mock sword fight. He could hardly have been five years old. As he grew, Seth became very loyal to Eva, enjoying her quiet ways and her wit. He would attach himself to her when she was in court and would miss her when she left.

"Come, his light is still on; the owls sent me notice as you were coming up the valley. He knows you are coming."

"The owls can send to you?" Eva was fascinated by the way the animals in which people's minds had been trapped were now deeply connected to their human selves. This meant that they could send through their minds. It was the opposite of what the serpents had meant to happen. Perhaps, she thought, that is all that sending really is, the ability to deeply connect with other living things, especially those you are drawn to. Eva always noticed her difficulty in connecting with reptiles, but mammals she sent to without any resistance at all.

Eva and Seth made their way down a set of spiral stairs and through a small, oak door. This led to the main corridor where the King's quarters were. Two guards stood outside the large, double oak doors. They had been refinished. They now just bore the King's crest with oak leaves and acorns. No trace of the serpents remained. Eva wondered if The Magician had helped do this, or if, with Lola taming the serpents, it had happened by itself. Seth noticed Eva looking at the carvings.

"All back to normal," he said. "Go in, he is waiting for you."

Eva walked through the doors as the guards pulled them open. The King sat with his back to her, gazing at the fire with a goblet in his hand. At his feet lay the beautiful silver-grey hunting hound, Lance, who raised his head more in respect than from being on guard.

The King turned his head. "Eva, you have been sent out late for good reason, I hope." The King gestured for her to sit down on the adjacent chair. "Have some mead to warm you." He poured the golden liquid from a crystal carafe. He then filled his own glass half way and added what looked like tea from a small jug.

"I'm getting used to having Milly's tea mixed with everything I drink." He smiled.

"Does Lance have it too?" asked Eva. "He looks most splendid." Eva put her hand down to stroke Lance's head and gently massage his ears. His coat almost sparkled in the fire light.

"He is very well indeed." The King also gave Lance a stroke. "When I am in good form, so is he. We seem to share every mood, every thought. I'd be lost without him. He is part of me. He kept me alive, though I don't know if the serpents intended that. Yet there is part of his consciousness that is just a dog. So we have to walk, play sticks, hunt. Of course, all of this is an excellent way to keep me in good health and spirit."

"That is just as well because we might need your

robustness," said Eva, before continuing to explain. "There was a small shipwreck on the coast of our valley. The gulls came up to The Magician's cottage while I was readying it for his return. They told me of this shipwreck and that there were two survivors. I went to investigate and unfortunately got shot in the wing. That's healed now, but the two castaways have arrived at my brother-in-law's farm. The Magician recognised them immediately. One is the daughter of his old friend, a woodsman. The other is the daughter of our neighbouring warlord who will not take lightly to her disappearance to our realm, if he knows where she has gone. The Magician suggests reinforced patrols go out to the shore to be certain we don't get any unwanted visitors."

"Mmm." The King was pensive. "I also know of this warlord. He calls himself the Serpent Lord. He is a doer. Everything in their world is about doing, making things bigger. Progress they call it. Yet there are poor people in his realm. Very poor, and rich, very rich. Much richer than I am, and I am the wealthiest person in our valleys, I would suppose. The society they come from is all about obtaining, not preserving. They constantly fight against the forces of nature rather than working with them. They also fight against anyone who may pose a threat, before asking questions." The King stopped and looked down at his hands. They were like any other man's hands, he just happened to be a king.

"Surely, this warlord could have come and caused

trouble at any time, yet a boat with his daughter in it was able to pass through to our land. Is this because the Forest Queen is not in her valley?" asked Eva.

"The Forest Queen may have been protecting the valleys in many ways. It is very hard to tell how vulnerable we might be without her there. It would, as The Magician says, be very prudent to line our shores with patrols. I also think that we should, in trying to extend the hand of friendship, get a message to this lord that his daughter is safe and well, and will be looked after until she can be returned."

"It is becoming very cold and stormy now. Trying to get a message to the lands beyond our valleys will be very difficult, even if I were to fly as a raven or run as a wolf. I also don't know if my ability to change will extend beyond these valleys. I could be caught out in the cold, and then there is Lola of course."

"She knows of you?" The King sounded both surprised and excited.

"Yes, yes, she has become so advanced so quickly that we thought it best. She will begin to notice all kinds of powers and have little understanding of what they are. I must give her the first level of training between the solstice and the equinox. I will need Ellery to support us for that, so his fast walking, which he shouldn't be doing at his age anyway, is not an option. Without the training she needs, the role she must play in the future might never be realised."

"That leaves my knights." The King stood up and paced in front of the fire.

Lance sat up, whining and trying to send. *"The owls, the owls could get there,"* he suggested.

The King then continued the train of thought in speech. "The owls can fly a long way, but I'm not sure if they could go up over the pass."

"What about the sea?" asked Eva. "Could Seth sail within safe distance around the end of the Eastern Valley and, from there, allow his owl to bring a message?"

"I don't know what would happen if Seth got too far from his owl self. They often go further from each other than Lance and I, but I feel for him when this happens. You can always see him looking out for the owl until the owl returns. Lance never goes any further than Milly's cottage from me. I don't pretend to understand how Seth and I have this connection with our animals. When I was in Lance, I could quite happily roam from myself, but now that I am in myself again, I find it very uncomfortable to be separated from him."

"How many days sailing is it to the warlord's land?" asked Eva.

"I would guess the journey there and back should take no more than three days," replied the King.

"Then we are not leaving ourselves exposed through the night of sun-return, which is most important. Everyone should be back where they are at the moment, keeping the balance between the valleys as best as we can."

"Yes, that is important." The King paused in thought. "I know of a very skilled sailor. Lars lives with his sister at the tavern on the beach. He could take Seth. Seth's owl mate could track them via the shore. It may seem very strange for an owl to fly out over the sea that far, but Seth's owl need only drop a written message and swoop out of the way again. Lars would have the boat turned and heading for home before it was unrolled."

Eva got up and walked to the western facing window. She opened it a slither to breath in the night air. There was a distant chill, one that would make the journey over the pass too dangerous in the night. But winter was not upon them from the south. The winds felt kind.

"The boat is the best option," she said. "Shall we discuss it further in the morning? I've no doubt there is an empty bed somewhere in the castle. The chill in the air would make flying over the pass near impossible for a small owl."

"The Magician's favourite room is always ready for a visitor," smiled the King.

Eva smiled back. "Then I bid you good night. Shall we breakfast at dawn? I think then I could manage to get a raven over the ridge in the light of day."

The King nodded.

Eva left the room knowing exactly where to go. As she passed through the lower corridor's reception area she encountered a large ball of fur settled in front of a waning fire.

Thomas looked up.

"*Hello, old friend,*" Eva sent. Then she saw two more

little heads appear from under Thomas's fluffy tail and paws.

"*Grand-kits*," Thomas sent back and smiled at Eva with his eyes.

"*Very fine.*" Eva bent down and gave Primo and Bella a stroke each. They stretched their legs and paws and then retracted back into little balls that seemed to reattach to Thomas. Eva stroked Thomas and then was on her way, down the corridor, past the laundry and into the west facing bedroom with the mahogany furniture.

The curtains were drawn. For a moment she considered opening them, but no, there was no sunset to see now. She would sleep, discuss the details of the voyage with the King so she could report back to The Magician, and then be on her way. She belonged to the Western Valley this time of year. This was only a brief interlude.

CHAPTER 7

A Message Sent

The Magician was true to his word and returned to the farm in the morning. Lola had helped keep watch over the two young women in the night, but she dozed most of the time, dreaming of being in her chair at the cottage with Pixey on her lap. She still longed for normality after her adventure in the Middle and Eastern Valleys.

The suggested mixture of balsam and honey had eased Ariella's cough, and both she and Morgan had slept soundly.

When The Magician arrived at the farm he seemed pleased with the progress the girls had made in the night. He was happy to continue to leave them in the care of Stella and Caitlin.

As Lola was being helped onto Coal by her brother, she heard The Magician say to her father, "Keep the girls' presence here quiet. If anyone strange comes asking, send someone up to me. I will, of course, put my normal watchers on guard, but they don't always understand the complexity of things. I may be all the way up the hill, but I will know you are coming and meet you half way." The Magician shook hands with Lola's father and turned to take Coal's reigns.

Lola's father then came around to Coal's side. He reached up and took Lola's hand. "We're proud of you, Lola," he said. "Very proud."

Lola smiled. "Thanks," she said quietly, quite unprepared for her father's words. It was all she could think of to say, and it was all that was needed.

They made very good progress up the hill, which surprised Lola. The Magician didn't seem to need to ride. He was as strong and steady on the rocky path as Coal.

Pixey was glad to see Lola, and Leo was relieved. Pixey had been pining. Lola scooped up Pixey and went to sit in her chair. The Magician followed her in. "Rest now, Lola," he said. "Chores can wait. I'll see to Nanny. You've had little time to recover from the night of the dead. You and Pixey need some time."

Lola sighed with relief. Yes, she just wanted to stop and cuddle Pixey for a day or two. She was sure that The Magician wouldn't be saying this without there being a good supply of soup on hand. She settled down further in her chair, gently stroking her dear little friend just on the small stripes on her forehead.

*   *   *   *   *   *   *   *

The King signed his name, Makram - King of the Three Valleys, and rolled up the scroll. He then bound it with his seal, the acorn and oak leaf, before giving it to Seth.

Seth rode his red mare down the rough road to

the Middle Valley's bay. There was a flat beach with a few houses and a tavern surrounded by cliffs on both sides. The Western and Eastern Valleys showed little life on their cliffs and shores. This was intentional. The Middle Valley was where the King could welcome travelers that were friends and also deter invaders. The other valleys had few places for boats to land on shore, as Morgan and Ariella had found out. High cliffs protected the Eastern Valley and rough rocky terrain under the water near the beach deterred easy landings in the Western Valley, although it was not impossible.

Lars was one of the King's best sailors. He had a single masted spristle cutter. Journeys along the coast in any weather were routine for him, but rarely did he have company and never the escort of an eagle owl. He hardly ever went beyond the headland of the Eastern Valley. Attention from the warlord, or the Serpent Lord as he was known because of his obsession with the creatures from which he took his name, was not something to be sought out.

"We have a window of calm weather for the next day or two," Lars said as Seth led his horse to the front of the tavern. He predicted the weather from a deep feeling in his bones and followed his knowledge of the cloud patterns in the sky. "My sister will look after the horse. We should not be gone too long." Lars was running a rope line through his hands, checking for frays. "This should do," he said to himself as he began to coil the line around his arm.

A slim woman, colourfully dressed and with the

same blue-grey eyes as Lars appeared on the porch of the tavern. "I will take her," she said, as she reached for the horse's reigns from Seth. A black hunting dog appeared with her, wagging his tail. "Come Arthur," said the woman to the dog. "You can help too." They disappeared into the stables.

"No time to waste." Lars hopped down off the porch. His compact but strong frame started making its way towards his boat. "The wind is with us, though it will be cold."

Seth, much taller than Lars, followed. They both waded into the shallows to embark a small wooden rowing boat that would take them to 'Gita', the boat named after Lars's sister. In some languages that means 'song'.

Lars rowed out the few hundred yards and secured the boat. Then they both climbed onto 'Gita'. Seth looked back at the land. Though late in the day, his owl was still breaking its normal routine to fly along with them.

"How close to the boat will he come?" asked Lars, noticing Seth scanning the land.

"While we are still on our own shores he will fly along them. But he knows he has to come to me when we reach the end of the headland of the Eastern Valley. Flying out so far over the water will be very strange for both of us."

"Hopefully that will be the quickest part of the journey. He can stick to land until we are just about to go around the headland. I will have to sail far out from it, though. The currents near the cliffs are dangerous."

Both men had their backs to the west. Both men had been distracted by the task at hand. Only Arthur the hunting dog noticed a boat similar to Lars's passing the cove and carrying on towards the Western Valley. The coast patrols were only just assembling in other places and thus far this boat had been undetected.

Arthur could not tell Gita this as she gave Seth's mare Red a bucket of oats, but he wanted to. He whined slightly, still looking out at sea.

"It's alright Arthur, just a new horse." Gita was still engaged in feeding Red and did not look Arthur's way.

Lars and Seth set off with the wind at their backs, a cold wind, but an agreeable one. It quickly took them in the direction they wanted to go. They sailed through the night on a steady course, having only to start tacking as they neared the cliffs in the Eastern Valley. The moon was waning and the night starry. Navigation was straight forward.

An hour before dawn they were about to pass the headland. "It's time." Lars said, tacking in and out of unseen currents that only he knew were there.

Seth called to his owl self, who he could feel circling with his mate at the start of the mountains in the Eastern Valley.

"Come, all will be well."

Seth's owl self circled a little way over the water. He called to his mate, a call of reluctance and confusion.

"Come to me. She will be waiting on our return," Seth sent again.

Seth's owl called out, not sending, but trying to express his displeasure through his cry.

"We can't linger," said Lars, knowing Seth was trying to lure the owl. Lars was now tacking far away from the cliffs trying to stay with the wind rather than being becalmed in the shadow of the mountains.

Seth felt the pull of the distance between himself and his owl. It was different to when his owl patrolled the Eastern Valley and he could picture everywhere that his owl self went. He felt himself going into an unknown place and his owl not understanding why they couldn't share the same vision. Seth's insides seemed to go into chaos. A feeling of sickness welled up in him, and then a churning of all of the muscles in his torso. His heart centre burned.

Owls make no noise when they fly. They are slower flyers than hawks. If a rabbit hears a hawk's wings then it is too late to run. She will be in the hawk's talons. But the rabbit won't hear the owl. She will simply feel the grip of the owl's claws into her sides.

Seth felt his owl's talons dig into his shoulder and then ease a bit so as not to draw blood. Seth's heart settled and he helped his owl adjust itself onto his gloved arm. Seth then turned his back to the wind and held his owl in close.

"Not far, friend. We will see her and our lands in a matter of hours."

As they rounded the headland, the dawn was starting. The emerging sun threw light across the water giving it a silvery grey hue. They could see an arid landscape on the distant shore framed by high snow-covered peaks. It seemed colourless compared to their valleys.

Owls make no noise when they fly, even when delivering a scroll. The guard at the dark marble arches to the Serpent Lord's palace only heard the thud of the scroll being dropped at his feet. Seth's owl was high above him and returning to the boat before the guard had stood up again.

Seth held out his arm as he saw his owl soaring back towards the boat. He had seen what the owl saw. The guard had picked up the scroll. That was all they could do. Lars was already turning the boat around for home. They hoped it would be that simple.

When the Serpent Lord opened the scroll he didn't feel much. The problem of his daughter, who was constantly refusing his choice of suitors, was happily out of his way for the moment. His daughter wasn't actually the girl that concerned him in The Three Valleys. He was interested in the girl that could talk to serpents. He tossed the scroll in a small brassier near his table in his quarters and watched it burn. It had been unimportant information really, except that they were aware that he might venture to their shores.

CHAPTER 8

Taken

The Serpent Lord didn't always hire very nice men. In fact mostly he hired very nasty men. They often were not very bright either. The three men he hired to search for his daughter were quite reckless. They had no fear of the winter seas and were quite happy to take the risk for a high enough price.

They had been told that there were three girls that they should look for: the two that were missing from his court, and a third, a girl with reddish-blonde hair who would be living with an old man. This one was much more important to the Serpent Lord. Goodness knows how the value of his own daughter might be seriously called into question now that she had been out of his sight and missing from court for so many days. She would be near worthless to him now. She was damaged goods, so the third girl was the most important one to bring back. If the other two could not be found, then so be it.

When they walked past the farm of Lola's family they only looked for a short while. "Just a farm," one said in gravely voice, "nothing here. Let's keep going up the hill." The protection The Magician had put around it quickly made them lose interest. The Magician's scouts took no action.

At The Magician's cottage, Lola had had a few days' rest and was feeling more settled in herself. She was enjoying showing Pixey some of the area around the cottage, especially Nanny's stall. Pixey was getting used to Nanny's milk and thriving on it.

It was an unusually warm day for late autumn. Pixey was playing with pieces of straw near Coal's stall. Lola was changing Nanny's bedding and Leo was dozing in a small spot of sun behind the cottage. The Magician had gone for a short wander to forage for a few last mushrooms.

It was very easy. After watching the cottage for about half an hour, one of the men stepped into Nanny's stall. Lola heard a rustle and then smelled something astringent and sharp. Then she blacked out.

Pixey was lounging on Coal's back. She saw two large men running across the front of the cottage. One had Lola over his shoulder.

"*MA!*" she sent with all of her might. Then she remembered Ma was far away. She tried to send to Lola but there was nothing, only blackness, thick impenetrable blackness. Lola's mind was closed. "*Ma,*" she sent again, this time digging her claws into Coal's back. He had also been dozing. He whinnied.

"*Coal - Lola's gone. Ma, two big men have taken Lola.*"

"*Send to The Magician little one, not your Ma, she's miles away.*"

"*I can't send to people when I'm so little and so upset.*"

Only to Lola, but she's gone. I can't smell her like she said." At this, Pixey jumped off Coal and tried to run after Lola's smell.

Even though she was still only learning to send, Leo had picked up Pixey's thoughts and was sprinting around to the front of the cottage after her. He ran over her, in his hurry to catch her and with one paw cupped around her, stopped her in her tracks.

"No you don't, but do send to Sophie to tell Lance. If Lola has been taken, the King must know."

"Ma," Pixey tried harder than ever. She had only managed to send to Sophie once since she had been at the cottage and that was with Lola's help. *"Two bad men have taken Lola, bad men, they smelled bad. We can't send to her, her mind is gone, tell Lance."*

Sophie was sitting on her bed in Milly's cottage. Pixey's desperate cry jolted her out of a mood of contemplation. Lola taken. *"By who?"* Sophie sent back.

"Bad men, big men. Tell Lance." Pixey was sending this as Leo carried her by the last of her kitten skin at the back of her neck and deposited her back in Coal's stall.

"Don't go anywhere," Leo warned Pixey. *"I'll go and find The Magician."*

Pixey hardly registered what Leo said, but Coal did and nudged Pixey into one corner at the back of his stall to guard her.

Sophie was up and out of her special door that Seth had made for her that led to the back of the cottage.

She jumped through Milly's pots and onto the ridge of the roof. Now that she was fit again, this was the quickest way to the castle from Milly's cottage. *"What did they look like? Smell like?"* Sophie sent back to Pixey as she scampered over the rooftops.

"Salty, fishy. Something like a snake on one arm." Pixey had only seen the back of one man's arm as he carried Lola away. The other had been in front of him. *"Tell Lance,"* Pixey pleaded. *"He will get Lola; he will bring her back soon."*

"I will tell Lance," promised Sophie. *"Stay safe, Little Three. Who is with you?"*

"Coal, I'm with Coal in his bed."

"Stay there, do not go anywhere by yourself. Hide in Coal's hay."

Sophie continued rushing over the rooftops and on to the ledges of the wall of the main part of the castle. She would seek out Seth. He had become one of her favourites. He would sense her urgency and find Lance.

Luck had it that a window on the western corridor had been left open. People were still being very forgetful about many things. This time it was in Sophie's favour. She ran along the corridor and, sure enough, found Seth sitting with Lars in front of a fire. They were resting and reflecting on their journey around the headland to the Serpent Lord's realm.

Sophie started rubbing up against Seth, purring loudly. She nudged and prodded him as hard as she could to try to give him the message that she had something to say.

"Did you miss me, little friend?" Seth picked Sophie up and scratched her chest as he often did. Sophie bit him.

"Ow - no, gentle," he warned.

Sophie jumped down and started prodding him again, walking in circles.

"That cat is a bit mad," chuckled Lars.

"Strange, she's usually very composed," said Seth.

Sophie's frustration grew. She then did something she knew was completely forbidden and would banish her from the castle under normal circumstances. She started to howl and yelp and went over to one of tapestries and started to claw at it.

"No, no that's special, Sophie." Seth tried to shoo her away.

Sophie ran a little away and then returned to repeat her behaviour only to be shooed again.

"She's trying to tell you something," said Lars, calmly filling his pipe and lighting it.

"I do miss Lola sometimes," Seth said.

At Lola's name Sophie jumped up on Seth's lap and purred even more loudly.

"I know, I know, we all miss Lola." Seth was trying to control Sophie's desperate prodding of him. "Oh, I think Lance and the King are down in the garden. Perhaps Lance could understand what you are on about." Seth started to get up.

Sophie could understand the words 'Lance' and 'garden'. She flew off of Seth's lap and back down the corridor to the open window. Seth barely saw where she had gone. By the time he had made his way down the back stairs to the garden gate, Sophie was sprinting across the gardens to Lance.

"Lola is taken, Pixey says bad men, they smell of salt and fish, very bad men, her mind is gone. There is a serpent on one of their arms."

Lance stopped dead in his game with the King. The King also instantly understood Sophie's message through Lance.

"No, no we sent a message." The King turned and saw Seth coming towards him. "You saw the guard pick up the message and bring it into the Serpent Lord, did you not?"

"Yes, why?" asked Seth now realising that Sophie indeed had been trying to tell him something.

"Sophie says that Lola has been taken," replied the King.

Sophie relayed more to Lance as Pixey kept sending her thoughts to Sophie. Leo had gone to get The Magician. Coal was guarding Pixey. Everything had been lovely up to that moment. Then Lola was gone. Pixey's heart was breaking. She kept meowing - Sophie could feel it.

"Seth, get Marcus and a few other men. Get over the pass to The Magician's Valley as soon as possible. I'll lead another set of men down to the harbour. Tell Lars we may need his services again. They can't have gone far."

*   *   *   *   *   *   *   *

Leo ran up the mountain path faster than he ever had in his life, all the time sending to his master. The Magician had only intended to be gone for an hour. He'd felt a little uneasy leaving Lola, but knew that anyone would have to come past her father's farm first and that his scouts would immediately send to report anything unusual. Only they didn't, as they had not noticed anything unusual.

"Lola, no, no!" The Magician's fast walking turned into running. He took strides longer than his own height as he flew down the mountain at superhuman speed.

"Go protect Pixey!" he sent to Leo.

Leo stopped. Yes, his master had picked up his message. He was coming back down the mountain. Leo turned and ran back towards the cottage. He could soon hear Pixey's mewing. He ran into Coal's stable. Leo began to wash her and purr loudly. *"Stay in control little friend, don't do this, we need to be strong now."*

"My feelings in me are exploding. Lola is gone. There is no Lola's mind, just blackness, thick sticky blackness." Pixey mewed.

The Magician too tried with all of his might to link with Lola's mind, but there was nothing, nothing that could get her to respond. But there was presence; she was alive, that at least he could determine. He could feel Pixey's desperation in his own efforts to try to connect with Lola.

He sent to Leo. *"Tell Pixey she is alive, her mind is clouded, but she is alive. I will find her. Tell Pixey I will bring her back."*

Running long distances with heavy loads is something that the two men did often. They could have run much further than the twelve miles down the valley with a load as light as Lola. Downhill was easy, especially with a reward that was so high. They managed to keep a mile ahead of The Magician, who was tiring as he came to the bottom of the ravine that opened up onto the deserted beach. They had already caught the tide and were on the horizon as the Magician met the water's edge.

The Magician dropped, exhausted and despondent to his knees. He dug his hands into the sand and then brought his fists into the air, squeezing the granules and then pulling his hands and the sand through his wild hair. He screamed to the disappearing boat on the horizon, "No! No, oh Lola, I'm so sorry. No, please, no!" His energy was spent. He crumpled in a heap on the sand. A seagull landed next to him. Eva's hand then rested on his shoulder. The Magician looked up.

"Tears," she said gently as she wiped them away from the old man's eyes.

The Magician hadn't been so knowingly and completely lacking in composure in front of anyone since he could remember. He was glad it was Eva, who he knew forgave him everything.

"I'll follow," she said. "I'll do what I can."

"But you're…" The Magician started to speak, but Eva stopped him.

"I'll be careful." And she was away.

CHAPTER 9

Hidden in Darkness

Eva followed. She circled over the boat; there were three men, one had been guarding the boat, and they did indeed have serpents tattooed to their forearms. Only the tops of their heads were visible to Eva, not their faces. Their hair was greasy and unkempt. They wore clothing made of leather and gold rings on their fingers. The Serpent Lord had many men like this in his employment, men for hire. "They would deliver their cargo," she thought as she circled the boat, "but why Lola?"

Eva flew down as close as she dared. Lola was breathing and moving slightly. Her little collapsed body looked as if it had been discarded at the bottom of the boat. One of the men noticed her stir. He took out a small phial and poured some liquid onto a filthy rag before covering Lola's nose and mouth with it. Her body went limp. Eva tried to sense what it was: opium. "Oh, please no," she thought. "Not too much."

Eva tried to penetrate Lola's mind. Nothing. Then she decided upon a different course. Instead of attempting to pull Lola's consciousness towards her, she followed it.

"Stay away Lola. Stay far away in the shadows. Don't

come back until you are away from these wretched men. Go to that place you found on the night of the dead. Stay there until you are safer."

The blackness of her mind was almost pleasant to Lola. She embraced it, feeling secure. It was when holes started appearing in it that she became disorientated, almost like there were wobbling prison bars with colour showing through. But Eva was telling her to walk away, find another way out. Eva was the only one she could sense. No one else. But she trusted Eva. She walked away from the blackness and the distorted colours. She walked back towards the field that she had seen her mother in. She would try to stay with her mother. There was no Isis, no Pixey this time. But surely her mother would protect her. She kept walking in the field, trying to stay as focused as she had whilst creating the boundary with the circle of light around the serpents' well.

* * * * * * * *

Marcus and Seth made their way with six other men up through the forest trails as the sun was just about to set. The winds were beginning to whip down through the trees from the higher peaks. Winter was closing in and they were risking getting stuck in the Western Valley.

Aya went part of the way. She relayed the message that Lola had been taken to other foxes and badgers so that they could be on the lookout for the intruders.

When it came time for Aya to turn back, she ran in front of the horses to catch their attention. They stopped and then the stag walked out of the woods as if to say, I will escort you now. Thus the animals followed and scented the woods to either side of the track sending the message to be on the lookout. The owls followed overhead.

"Please, please," Marcus kept saying to himself, "let them have come this way. Nature will betray them and they'll never suspect it."

But dawn came, windswept and with freezing rain, yet no sign of Lola. Seth, Marcus and their group of companions arrived at The Magician's abandoned cottage feeling quite dejected.

Leo crept cautiously out of the barn. He recognised Marcus and Marcus's horse. He rubbed up against Marcus's leg, who bent down to stroke him. Leo skidded away from Marcus's touch and made his way back to the barn.

"Seth," Marcus said, turning to his brother, "can your owl self make out anything Leo might be able to tell us?"

Seth's owl and mate were resting in nearby trees. This wasn't a good time for them, as they slept through most mornings.

"I can get a sense," Seth said. In his mind he called upon his owl self who pulled away from his branch and circled the yard, trying to pick up from Leo a visual account of what had happened.

Seth turned back to Marcus. "They carried Lola

down the valley. She was hanging lifeless over the shoulder of a tall dark man who smelled of fish. The Magician followed some time later. No one has come back. Pixey and Coal are in the barn."

Marcus went over to the barn and slowly opened the door. In the dim light he could see the back of Coal.

"You're alright, aren't you, good man?" Marcus walked to the side of the horse and stroked his back. Coal made a noise at the back of his throat to acknowledge Marcus.

Pixey was cold and hungry. She began to mew. Marcus followed the sound. He bent down and scooped her still very small self into his hands.

"We had better feed and rest everyone as best we can for a few hours," said Marcus, feeling at a loss after finding so little to go by. His bond with Lola seemed only a memory now. "Come little cat, you need food." He held Pixey to his chest and went into the cottage.

The men stoked the fires and ate their provisions. They ate some but not all of The Magician's soup. Pixey was given warm goat's milk and bread, which she devoured having gone almost a whole day without food. The horses were fed and watered.

Seth kept trying to decipher anything important from his owl's perspective. Marcus walked around the cottage gently holding and stroking Pixey, who had settled now. She was quite sure that Marcus would take her to Lance and that Lance would take her to Lola.

Marcus noticed the small pine railing that helped steady the climb up to Lola's loft space. Lola had carefully tied the green and purple ribbons that Marcus had given her in a criss-cross pattern around it. He remembered how she had used those ribbons to form the bond between them when they were approaching the Forest Castle. 'Sometimes you have to double your feeling of a bond when the other person is not able to do so,' he thought.

Marcus turned towards the rest of the men. "We rest for an hour and then we go. We must find The Magician and we must find Lola."

* * * * * * * *

Eva tried to follow the boat around the cliff's edge to the sea bordering the Middle Valley and the Eastern Valley. The wind was howling down through the small fishing port of the Middle Valley. She watched as the men skillfully tacked the boat in and out of the strong winds. Yes, they were experienced sailors. They had a payment to collect and they would do this right.

The winds became too strong for Eva to keep tracking the boat. They had sailed the boat further out to sea, where the going was smoother. Further than she dared to go. She knew that if she followed there was no way of guaranteeing her return.

"*Stay in that place, Lola, travel deep within your mind,*" she tried to send. She then turned and headed diagonally into the wind. She managed to come to rest on a partially protected cliff. It was still too high to climb down as herself. She hovered down about another fifty feet and then changed back. Following Lola all the way had too many dangers as a seagull. She saw where they were going. She would tell the King when he arrived on the beach. She had been a seagull for too long for it to be safe. She needed rest.

It took about half an hour for her to feel steady on her feet again. She slipped off the shale ledge and started to make her way towards the lights of the tavern nearest the beach.

"A warm drink and a corner to doze in for an hour or so, please," she requested as she walked through the tavern doors.

Gita was tidying the bar area as Eva walked in. Gita smiled, "Of course, on the King's fare?" Gita had noticed Eva's ring. The King made regular payments to all of the taverns in the Three Valleys so his troops and advisors could always have what they needed without having to carry an excess of provisions. Eva's ring had a small version of his acorn seal. This was a sign of her importance to his court and that she should be served whatever she needed wherever she went.

"He may be here soon himself. There has been trouble."

"I see," said Gita, knowing that to ask why would be seen as inappropriate but thinking that it probably had something to do with her brother's voyage with Seth. She handed Eva a large terracotta mug filled with a blend of Milly's tea, honey and hot milk. Eva had not yet tasted Milly's tea. It took some getting used to but, after a few sips, it was quite palatable.

"You can have a bed," offered Gita.

"No, thank you." Eva sat in the window seat arranging herself as comfortably as she could against some sheepskins that were draped there. "I want to keep watch on the weather and the beach."

"Suit yourself." Gita left a small single lamp burning on the bar and retired up the back stairs of the tavern.

A storm howled for much of the second half of the night. Eva rested, but never really slept. By dawn she could hear men's voices and horses outside. Then she heard Lance's bark. Her hunch that the King and some of his men would be arriving was being realised. She went to the tavern door and called out. Lance immediately appeared, bounding around the corner of the building. The King and two other men followed. They entered the bar area where Eva had been harbouring from the storm.

"She's been taken east," Eva explained. "I couldn't follow because of the winds, though they were very adept sailors and I think they will complete their voyage. I can only guess that they were hired to take Lola. She is nothing like the Serpent Lord's daughter. They couldn't have got the two girls confused."

"It's a mystery," said the King. "We sent word that the girls were safe and we would arrange safe passage home when weather permitted and they were fit to travel."

One of the men with the King was Lars. "Our boat

was seen from their shore. The message was picked up by the guard and taken straight into the palace. No one followed us."

"That is because these men had already been sent," said Eva. "There is a chance that Lola's taming of the serpents in our valleys has had an effect on the serpents elsewhere. They work on the subconscious. That is how they entrap people. Even if Lola has harnessed them in our realm, they may still be causing a stir elsewhere. The underworld has many outlets throughout the world."

"But how would they know of Lola and what would they want from her?" asked the King.

"How? I do not know. What do they want? That is simple," Eva explained. "She is young, unformed and yet powerful. They want her power before she has control of it herself."

"Do they know of her power?" asked the King.

"Maybe partially, but hopefully not enough to get what they want."

The King turned to Lars. "We must go after her. Make three boats ready. Even with this weather, we must get through."

"No, wait," said Eva, putting her hand on the King's arm to check his determination. Lance whined slightly feeling as if he too was being stopped in his pursuit.

"I have sent Lola deep inside her own mind. She will not reemerge until she is pulled out by a stabilizing animal, possibly one than can help and keep her safe. In the meantime, we need to concentrate on distracting the serpents, which means drawing them to the well in the Forest Castle. This will ensure that they cannot be influenced from another well. When the weather improves I can scout, possibly with Seth. Lars can too. We need to bring The Magician back to the castle, the girls too. We need them all in one place for their own protection. Then we can make our way to the Forest Castle. Trying to steal her back might be the most dangerous option for both her and us at the moment. I sense that the Serpent Lord wants confrontation and I for one am not prepared to give him what he wants."

The King looked out at his troops that he had brought with him. This seemed too passive, but he trusted Eva. He knew Marcus and Seth would return within a day, probably with The Magician if they hadn't found Lola.

Lance now put his paw on the King's knee. *"I sense that Eva is right. I want to go and find her now, but I sense Eva is seeing beyond this."*

The King turned to the other two men. "Tell the men to ready themselves to return to the castle with anyone who isn't particularly needed in the village." He looked back at Eva and Lars. "We have no idea what this Lord is up to. I want the beach guarded, and no one vulnerable left here."

Both men nodded formally and returned to the troops outside.

The King turned towards Eva. "Can you get back around the coast to let the others know of our meeting and plans?" he asked.

Eva nodded. She hoped she had rested enough.

The King then walked out with Eva to Lars. "Lars," he said, "I will ask you to stay here with a small company of men. Others might join you in a day or two with further instructions."

"Of course," said Lars respectfully.

Eva looked out onto the sea. The storm was moving west. It wouldn't be long before she could follow it safely. Yet, more bad weather seemed to be appearing on the Eastern horizon. She would have to make her escape to the west swift.

CHAPTER 10

Oskar

Oskar was the product of two of the Serpent Lord's favourite hunting dogs, only they weren't supposed to have mated. Others in the litter looked like his retriever mother or his curly haired father and were farmed out to lesser scouts and hunters for companionship, but Oskar just didn't look like anything but himself. In centuries to come, he would become a sought after breed, but in Oskar's time he was simply seen as a mistake. He was given to one of the prison guards as he was very boisterous and had an echoing bark. Even the smallest stirring of movement would send him barking, though he was quite friendly with it.

Oskar was particularly fond of children. He was concerned by the young girl who was curled up in a heap at the back of one of the cells. She was breathing, but she was off somewhere else in her mind. He knew she had been upstairs. He didn't know what was upstairs, but the guards who took her there seemed very cross when they dragged her back down again.

There was another dog too. She was behind the bars of another cell. She was beautiful. Her long graceful face and speckled blue-grey eyes enchanted him. But, like the dark-skinned man in the cell with her, she was very sad.

"I've lost my girl," she explained, *"and now my man is in trouble because another girl was lost at the same time. We were about to go and look for them. The boat was ready, but a piece of paper fell out of the sky that made the Lord very angry and we were put in here."*

Oskar couldn't make any sense of what this beautiful dog, who said her name was Sona, was talking about.

The cells were a grim place. All kinds of people came and went. He was always praised for noticing them. But they were only ever sad or frightened or angry. Often they would just disappear and he would never see them again. He had no idea why. His world was very small.

Oskar was looking at the girl now. He wondered if this was the girl that Sona lost. He tried to describe the girl to Sona, but Sona said that this girl wasn't anything like her girl.

So, Oskar sat by the cell, hour after hour, and wondered about this girl. He started to feel a strong link with her. He felt it stronger than he usually did with humans. Certainly more than he felt with his guard. He tried his best with his guard, but got very little response, unless he barked because he noticed one of the sad, frightened or angry people doing something. Oskar's mother told him to always be patient with humans. Always try to be affectionate. Some humans just didn't quite know how to be these things and it was up to the dog to draw out the kindness in them.

Sometimes though, she warned, it could go terribly wrong and humans would draw out nastiness in dogs. There were some dogs that were more susceptible to this than others. In their breed this was less common but, she warned Oskar, if he in any way was being trained to be nasty he must find a way to get far away from the human doing this. Even if it meant that he must go completely into the unknown. This was his mother's most earnest advice the night before her litter was moved on. He missed his mother. Being with just these humans meant that he had less stimulation and he could feel quite dull some of the time.

Having Sona to talk to cheered him, even though she wasn't very cheerful herself. He asked her about what was beyond the stairs and what was outside the small courtyard they let him play in on occasion. She talked about things like grass and interesting smells and playing sticks. She spoke of other strange sounding animals, like goats and sheep, who gave humans a white liquid called milk that they drank.

Sona, being a welcome addition to his life, made him feel more settled, but this girl, well she excited him. He could sense what was in her mind and she was in a place a bit like the one that Sona had explained, only greener. Not only that, if Oskar really concentrated, he could see where this girl was in his own mind, and he could join her. He could run with her and play sticks. He started to be able to smell things that were in this grassy place which were delicious to him and he could roll and scratch his back on patches of rocky soil.

So, Oskar sat, focused and quiet, and joined this girl in her mind. She wasn't eating or drinking, but he knew she was alright, a bit like the tortoise he remembered finding with his litter-mates in the Lord's garden in early spring.

Lola could not remember how she got back to the beautiful place where she had seen her mother. She did see glimpses of her mother now, but never quite as clearly as that night in Eva's cave. But now there was someone new. A dog. A blonde, curly-haired dog, with deep black eyes. He was a bit clumsy at first, but Lola managed to teach him to play with sticks. Soon he was an expert. His face always had a look of laughter in it, or love and concern. When he looked at Lola he looked clearly at her. Sometimes this would get him so excited that he rolled around on his back. She would then rub and tickle his tummy until he couldn't help himself and he would bark.

It was during one such session that the dog led Lola to the edge of the field. Although the sky was light in the field, it started to darken at the edges. Lola saw her mother briefly from the side as she followed.

"It's alright, I will keep you safe," she heard her mother say in a voice that was so like Eva's that she wondered if it was her.

Lola followed the dog. She climbed over a style into the black. Now she remembered the black. She almost liked it, it stood between her and the grisly presence of the men, and then she remembered the men who had taken her from Pixey. She could still hear Pixey's little voice trying to alert the others.

Lola moved. Every part of her was stiff. Her stomach churned then she felt it heave. She sat up retching. She threw up as she came to sitting. She shivered. At least vomiting made her feel a bit better.

There was a small whine from across the stone floor. There, behind a set of bars, sat the dog.

"Can we play sticks for real?" Oskar wiggled with excitement at the sight of Lola moving but, unlike his usual self, he didn't bark. He wanted Lola's attention, not the guards'.

Lola looked around. She lay on a sort of mattress stuffed with very rough and old straw. There was a dirty sheep skin half thrown over her, which she had been sick on. She pushed it away, slightly retching again.

"Water - over here - clean, won't make you sick." Lola heard the dog send. Water, fresh water, she hoped. She tried to stand but felt very dizzy. Her clothes were stiff and she realised they were caked with salt.

Lola crawled across the grey stone floor. It was cold and dusty, making her shiver from both the feel of it and the temperature. She sat beside the large tin bucket of water, almost hugging it. She splashed a little in her face and mouth. It tasted sweet enough, so she had a little more. As much as she dared.

"I'm Oskar." The dog put his paws through the bars. He managed to reach the tip of her toes on her outstretched foot. He so wanted contact with this girl. She had already shown him a life that he could not

have dreamed existed before his mind had mingled with hers.

"I'm Lola," Lola sent back. She had never imagined a more horrible place. It was dark, with only wisps of light coming through the spaces in the stone walls as they allowed a freezing draft. The iciness of winter was biting. The smell was like that of the slaughter shed on the bigger farm up the hill from her father's. She had only ever been in it once, vowing never to visit again. Only this place had a more putrid smell, as if something had died and no one had bothered to do anything with the remains.

"I'm Lola," she repeated, *"and I'm scared and lonely and I miss my kitten and my Magician and how did I end up here Oskar? What is this place?"* Tears now rolled down Lola's cheeks. Oskar's deep brown, compassionate eyes followed their path.

"It's a place for guards. That's what my man calls himself. He doesn't really call me by my name, just 'dog'. I know my name is Oskar because my mother told me that. We all had names, all of her pups." Oskar was now pressing his nose up against the bars of Lola's cell, reaching both paws towards her. *"Now you know my name, you can call me Oskar. I like having a name again; it feels like having your litter-mates back."*

"Where do those stairs lead to?" asked Lola, wiping her tears with her sleeve. Lola could see winding stone steps about ten feet from the bars of her cell. She had a faint memory of them and a large room that had a cathedral-like ceiling. This ceiling had spun and spun

as she looked up at it. She had been asked questions and a young boy had stood beside a grandly dressed, but coarse and angry, man - a lord of some kind. The boy had pages of paper in his hands and tears in his eyes. He was frightened, but steadfast. She admired him. They were asking Lola questions, but she couldn't respond. The large hall just kept spinning. Finally they gave up and dragged her back across to the door that led to the stairs.

Oskar mingled with Lola's mind. *"I have never gone up those stairs. I only know that they make humans angry, sad, or frightened. Sometimes they go up and never come back. That is when they seem the most frightened."*

"Has anyone ever been here for a very long time?" Lola asked.

"I first came here in the deep coldness and now it is getting like that again. No one has been here as long as me."

Lola looked down at Oskar's paws. She wished she could disappear into that inky blackness again. An ache came over her, starting at the centre of her chest then spreading down to her stomach and across her shoulders: fear, deep fear. She took a long breath and looked at Oskar again. His dark eyes carried only love and playfulness. How could he have been made a prison dog? Lola tried to stay in the moment of his caring eyes. She knew one moment of kindness was worth a hundred of cruelty and that she would gain strength if she just stayed focused on the beauty of those kind eyes.

"Love and fear are the two strongest human emotions, of the two, love is much stronger. But we often give in to fear, rarely giving love the chance to work at its fullest force." Lola remembered The Magician's voice in her mind. Of all of the things he said to her, this was one of the things he regularly repeated.

Lola reached her hand through the bars and stroked Oskar's head. She even managed a weak smile. *"Do you go out of the building any other way?"* she asked.

"I go down there." Oskar turned his head towards the dim tunnel leading away from Lola's cell. *"There is a little space to play and do my business. No grass. I would love to play in grass."*

"I'm sure you would." Lola was now stroking his head and ears. It was making her feel stronger, more grounded, as if she was shaking off something more than the opium. Eva, Eva had put her into this state until she could act with her wits about her. Now she remembered. But Eva had not been herself. Lola shuddered. That wasn't important now.

"Is there any way out of the place you play?" Lola asked.

"Yes, I came in that way. A huge gate with heavy bars, like these bars. The man opens them with smaller bars."

Lola was puzzled. She mingled her mind with Oskar's, trying to understand his description. She saw his memory. He was much smaller. A stout unshaven man in stained breeches led him through a pair of iron gates using a large key that bore the same design as the gates. Serpents - serpents twisted and entwined around the tops of the gates' bars. She felt Oskar's fear and apprehension, then his resolve to be brave, to try to transform his man like his mother had told him to do.

"Keys," Lola said out loud, then she sent to Oskar, *"They are called keys these small bars. They open gates and doors and things that are locked. Where are these keys, Oskar? Do you ever see them?"*

"They are on my man. They are attached to his clothes around his waist. He uses them to open everything."

"Do you know if those keys are the only ones? Does anyone else have those keys?"

Oskar thought for a moment. *"I have heard the same sound that they make, but I am not sure where. I need time to remember."*

Suddenly there was another mind. Very close. Lola knew that there must be other cells, but they were cleverly positioned to make it impossible to see anyone else's.

"Morgan, my girl," sent the someone. Someone else was trying to send to Lola. Someone who was drawn towards the ineffable bond between Oskar and Lola. Not because she wanted to be, but because she too had this kind of bond with another human.

"You have seen Morgan, my girl," the 'someone' sent.

Lola could now feel the other dog. She could picture the visual descriptions being sent. Lola was communicating with both dogs now, yet not making a sound.

"You must be Sona. Yes, I have seen your girl, Morgan,"

Lola sent.

"You are my girl now," Oskar sent.

"Even through the salt and the filth I can smell her on you a little," Sona sent.

It was a three-way conversation where they all knew each other's minds. But Lola felt something else too.

"We are here, Lola. The boy wrote about you, though he didn't know you were real like we did. We are real too. We are welcome here - the Lord, the Serpent Lord likes us…"

"Stop!" Lola pulled away from everyone.

Oskar got up in a start and backed off, frightened by Lola's sudden change.

Lola had let her mind become too open. She must guard her mind. Eva had helped her hide it but, in coming out of the spell, she had gone the other way. She needed to rebalance herself. She just focused on Oskar very clearly.

"I need time to find more stability in my mind. Tell Sona that I will talk soon, but only when I'm ready. There are beings here who would swallow up my mind if I let them. I will tell her about her girl soon. Morgan is safe. She is with my father. Tell her that. I must rest now."

Lola pulled away from the bars and curled into a ball against the rough stone wall. It felt cold on her back. She looked over at the dirty sheepskin. No, she couldn't face it. She would put up with the cold. She pulled her mind back from everything around her. It actually worked with more ease than she had ever experienced. She concentrated on Eva's cave - on just that one quiet, focused night. No one could have touched her. 'How do I bring my mind to that space now?' she asked herself. She reached out for help, but towards the sky. The serpents were underground; Eva had been in the sky. She had to send her mind upwards for help.

CHAPTER 11

Re-grouping

By midmorning it was safe for Eva to take to the skies again. She went as a seagull. She loved post-storm wind; strong enough to thrill, but safe enough to fly. The sea had taken on a turquoise colour with white tails highlighting it. The sun now hung low in the sky and caused the sea hue to be deep and rich.

Eva was tempted to try to send to Lola in her seagull form, but it was too risky. She would help by collecting everyone together first. Eva made her way up the Western Valley and saw the lone figure of The Magician clambering through the ravine. He must have spent the night on the beach hoping for the winds to drive the boat back, but they hadn't. He now seemed to be making his way to Lola's father's farm to tell him about her abduction.

Eva circled above and called out. The Magician stopped and gazed up at the marvel of how his apprentice had mastered changing with little but a bit of theory from him.

"I will find the others. Stay at the farm," Eva sent.

The Magician assented with a nod, not quite knowing what else he could do.

Eva flew further up the valley and sensed Seth's

owl. He was reluctantly flying from tree to tree, even though it was day.

"*Where are they?*" she asked.

"*Half a mile further up. I'll let them know you are coming.*"

Eva flew another quarter of a mile and then found a grassy patch to land on. She shook her feathers and then changed. Her arms were still stiff from the strong winds. She had been enjoying flying. Maybe too much. It was best to stay in her human form for a while. She started to meander her way up the path, knowing the others would appear soon.

It was the clop of Coal's hoofs that she heard first, then Marcus appeared from around the bend, leading him. Seth was close behind, leading the rest of the horses down the rocky path, followed by their men.

Marcus had a small sling around his shoulder and waist from which hung green and purple ribbons. Inside the sling, Pixey's ears poked out. As Eva walked up to Marcus, she could see Pixey's eyes, open and still in shock.

"What to do? What to do?" thought Eva. Should she use Pixey to try to reach Lola, or should she just let Pixey be with those who were familiar to her? Eva stroked Pixey's head.

"*She will come back,*" Eva sent.

"*I know; Lance will find her for me. Marcus is taking me to Lance,*" Pixey replied.

Eva sighed within. She would be so much more comfortable dealing with this from her retreat on the mountain, but maybe this time she had to overcome the challenge of working with others to solve this. She smiled at Marcus. "She thinks Lance will be able to find Lola," she said as she continued to stroke Pixey's head.

"Where is Lola, Eva?" asked Marcus, not really wanting to know the truth of it but not being able to keep from asking.

Eva turned towards the direction of the sea. "Beyond the Eastern Valley by now. Lance hasn't got a chance of getting there without a boat and fair weather, and neither have we. I put her in a deep meditative state. They won't get anything out of her and it's unlikely they will hurt her. Being in that state protects you. You are not fun to hurt because you don't respond. Also, the people who took her must know something about what she can do so they will be cautious to some extent. I don't believe she was taken by mistake in place of the Serpent Lord's daughter. These men knew what they were after."

Marcus felt his stomach churn. He tried to respond but his voice cut off. He looked down at Pixey and felt Coal beside him. A few days ago Lola's life had been that of a little girl with a beautiful kitten and a friendly goat. Now it was about others wanting to steal or corrupt her power. She had only just learned to find it within herself.

Marcus took a deep breath. "What do we do now?" he asked of Eva. Seth and the other men were quiet and listening now.

"We go to the farm, collect everyone together and

go back to the King's castle. Then a few of us go to the Forest Castle. It's the closest place of power from which we can try to connect with Lola and guide her back."

"How will she get back by herself?" Marcus was indignant at the thought they were not all jumping on a ship to follow and rescue her.

"She will find the right companion and will find a way. If we are there, I can guide her while The Magician controls the serpents in the absence of the Forest Queen. Lars is ready to go, but we must know more before we set off. I can only do that by getting closer."

Marcus looked back at Seth and his men. They looked on expectantly. Marcus simply nodded and they followed as they carried on down the path towards the farm.

When they arrived, the farmyard suddenly became a very busy place. The collie dog was barking, Pixey was growling at this sound, the horses were restless. Lola's brothers helped the men lead the horses over to another drink and a small meal. They had not been ridden so they were not too fatigued.

Indoors, Caitlin and Stella busied themselves by making more breakfast for the eight men. Eva sat with The Magician and Lola's father by the fire. Lola's father was pensive indeed at the news of her abduction. He looked towards the door to the room where the two girls were convalescing.

"Is it their doing, is this a trade off?" he asked. He

had never really known what to do for Lola, she was so different from his sons, but he loved her no less, perhaps more because she was so unique.

"I don't think so. It seems their landing on our shores is simply a strange coincidence," explained Eva. "They may help. The younger one particularly, I think, could tell us a lot about what we are up against in trying to get Lola back."

"Are they to stay here?" asked Lola's father. "The child of my daughter's captor as my guest?"

"No," returned The Magician. "We think it best to get them to the King's castle. You have no real protection here. If there is any retaliation, it is best it falls where there is some defense. No one need even know they have been here."

"Good," Lola's father grumbled and sighed. "What can I do? You can't expect me to just milk my cows and herd my sheep as if nothing has happened."

Eva and The Magician sat, quietly regarding Lola's father. He had not known about Lola's quest to the Forest Castle or about her undoing of the enchantment of the serpents while Lola had been away with The Magician in the Middle Valley. It had only been reported to him when they returned. He had just milked his cows and herded his sheep. Because of this, he created stability in the depths of Lola's consciousness. Because of this, she had been able to do what she did.

The Magician spoke. "Sir, with the greatest respect, that is exactly what we expect you to do. Lola will be reaching out for the ordinary to ground herself. If you are not here she may get confused and worried and not be able to cope with this challenge. Yet again, I'm afraid that much of what Lola needs to do to save herself is up to her. She will not be able to do this without stability. She has great power, she learns quickly. No ordinary girl could have spoken the words to bind and then silence the serpents of the underworld. No ordinary girl has been captured by the Serpent Lord. If she can tame the serpents, she can overcome the Lord."

"So you are just going to wait for her to work it out for herself?" Lola's father stood up as the anger in his voice rose.

"No." Eva reached out her hand and touched his. "No," she said again quietly. "I will go to the Forest Castle. It's the place from which I can guide her best and it is closest to the next valley over the mountains. The King is ready with a boat to go at any minute. But we must be clear what we are up against, for Lola's sake as much as for ours." Eva was now holding her brother-in-law's arm.

Lola's father collapsed back down into his chair. "So, I will milk my cows and herd my sheep and with every minute of the day feel the loss of Lola in my heart." Lola's father held his face in his large, gnarled hands as if they could shield him from the grief he was feeling.

Morgan and Ariella could hear all of the commotion in the farmyard outside their room. They were both much better following solid food and a good night's sleep. They had no idea of the goings-on that their shipwreck had caused across the valleys. They thought that they had simply been taken in by a kind farming family and that the local herbalist had been brought in to check on their welfare. Ariella was very pleased with this. She was fed up with being somebody. The Serpent Lord's daughter, who was bartered for the highest price by the flocking suitors. Although she suspected that her father did have kind feelings towards her, his love of power, money and status always stood between them. She was a commodity, just like everything else around him. He paid more attention to the young bard who told and wrote stories about magic and power and serpents under the earth. The only time his attention was on her was when she was dressed in her finest and could be shown off to the wealthy suitors, none of whom interested her in the least.

There was a quiet knock at the door. Caitlin, who had been on a constant vigil for them, wasn't there. Morgan answered first. "Come in," she said as she sat up further in bed. Her legs were still tired, but just beginning to feel that restlessness that one feels after an illness when life and energy begin to slowly return.

The door opened. It was the old man who had been there with the girl, Lola, a few days earlier.

"Good morning, Morgan, Ariella." He smiled a weak smile.

Ariella noticed how tired he looked, and unkempt compared to his last visit. Both girls looked beyond him, expecting to see Lola too, but he was alone. They liked Lola, who was obviously learning her craft and not yet much of a nurse, but a captivating free spirit. She had talked of her animal friends. This had particularly interested Morgan.

"No Lola?" questioned Morgan.

"No, no Lola," The Magician's voice cracked slightly at the saying of Lola's name. "I've come to see how you are and," he gently lifted Ariella's hand to check it's colour and felt her forehead as he spoke, "to see if you are fit to travel." The Magician then went over to check Morgan's temperature and colour as well.

"We are all to travel to the Middle Valley of our three valleys, to the King's castle. It is humble compared to your father's estate, Ariella, but we try to live simply." The Magician was now sitting down on the small chair at the end of the bed. "As far as I can see, you are both recovering well. If we bundle you up and give you a horse each, I think you could make the journey. How would you feel about that?"

"Are you going to hand me over to my father?" asked Ariella, surprised that The Magician seemed to have such clear knowledge of who she was and who her father was.

"At this point, no," The Magician replied. "The weather is too severe now. The snows will have started in the mountain passes and the sea would only be intermittently calm enough to sail. We have sent word that you are safe."

"How, if the weather has been so bad?" inquired Morgan. She was not interested in returning to the Serpent Lord's domain, but she did want to be reunited with her father and Sona. Spending a whole winter cooped up in some strange castle was not an attractive proposition to her. Then again, she thought, perhaps Lola will be there, and all of the animals she spoke of. "Will Lola be there? And Lance?" asked Morgan.

"Lola won't be there, no. Lance will be, but I'm afraid that Lola is not now in these valleys. She was taken very early yesterday. We think she was taken by your father, Ariella. We are not sure if she was taken because it was thought she was you or because of who Lola is."

"Anyone who works for my father knows exactly who I am," Ariella said, trying to dismiss the idea that her father would have wanted to take Lola in her own mind. "What makes you think she was taken by my father? He has all the herbalists and physicians he can use."

"The men who took her had serpents tattooed on their arms and serpents carved in the bow and trim of their boat. You see, Lola can talk to the serpents and we think that this might be of interest to your father," said The Magician quietly. His head was bowed down, looking at his folded hands and he slowly rubbed his thumbs against each other.

Ariella now looked down too; this did indeed sound like her father's men. The ones he sent to do things that he would never speak of in front of her. Then she thought about the night before she and Morgan set sail. He had been standing in his great hall beside his well. His well often bubbled and hissed with ethereal light and green mist, but it had been quieter recently. He was quizzing his young bard, who told him of a young witch who had tamed the serpents and gained power over them. He had told his guards that she must be found.

Ariella looked up at The Magician. "I think maybe you are right," she said quietly. "My father would have sent men to find the young witch who tamed the serpents. He was most displeased by the calming of his well and threatened to punish the young bard who told him the story, believing that in the tale being told it had become true."

The Magician smiled a kind but tired smile at Ariella. "That is what we suspected," he said.

"So, are you going to keep us as prisoners as long as they have Lola?" Morgan asked, now feeling very cross about their whole predicament. She wondered how she had ever let herself get pulled into this.

"No, you are not prisoners. In fact the castle doesn't even have a prison. You will be guests. In these valleys, if someone offends, we ask them to leave - sometimes never to return. No, you are neither prisoners nor exiles. We will simply look after you until we can return you to your home, if that is what you want." The Magician was now standing. "I'll ask Caitlin to help you prepare for the journey."

"But why? Why do we have to leave here?" asked Ariella.

"It is important that we can focus on getting Lola back. It will be much easier to care for you and protect you at the King's castle. Besides," and now The Magician smiled, "I think Lance would like to meet you too. He misses Lola." With that, The Magician left.

Ariella looked at Morgan. "It's you who wants to meet the dog. I just want to be as invisible as possible to anyone important," she scolded under her breath, but loud enough for Morgan to hear.

Morgan started getting out of bed. "He's not just any dog. He's a king and a dog at the same time and apparently very wise. Perhaps he can suggest how to get around being married off to the highest bidder."

* * * * * * * *

The party was ready by midday. Because of the late start, they would be travelling well into the night. With the horses they could take the road quickly and be over the highest part of the pass and down into the Middle Valley by sundown. Lola's father made sure they had plenty of spare torches and food for the horses.

Eva rode with them. Seth's owl would announce their arrival; she had already spent too long as a gull. She borrowed a horse from the farm. Marcus kept his satchel, with Pixey in it, around him all the while. She had eaten a small amount of stew mixed with goat's milk, but quickly got back in her satchel and stared out, willing everyone else to be ready to go so she could get to Lance, who she was sure would be able to find Lola for her. Marcus rode Coal as a comfort for her, having given The Magician his own horse.

Ariella and Morgan were given a space on the horses with two of the men, but with Eva right beside them to supervise. Thus they rode off, leaving Lola's father staring at the space they left, and grieving for the hole in his heart that Lola had left.

*　*　*　*　*　*　*　*

Lola could see the sky in her mind. She could feel the sky, but she wasn't following Eva. She was on the back of a huge brown bird circling over her father's farm and then turning up towards the mountains. Then she could feel Seth. She was with Seth's owl. She was flying over the procession. She looked closely; she could see The Magician, Eva, Marcus. Marcus had something wrapped around him. Small ears poked out of it. They carried Pixey with them.

Pixey was wary of the owl, as she was still small enough to be taken by one. Lola pulled back and led the owl away from her. She could see more. She could see her father standing in the farmyard, Caitlin trying to persuade him in. There was no way of telling him that she was still alive. But Seth, she could tell Seth through the owl. She tried to send to Seth's owl but it was very difficult. Why this owl, she thought? But then she got a sense that the owl had flown over the building she was now in. He was her only link, but not a very communicative link. She tried again, sending only, *"I'm okay, tell my father."*

Seth stopped.

Yes, Lola thought. She sent again. *"I'm okay. Tell my father."*

Eva and Marcus turned and looked at Seth, puzzled by his halt.

"It's Lola - she's talking to my owl self. She's okay." Seth then turned his horse back. "I'll catch you up, her father must know."

The Magician was moving slower than the others but heard what was said. He gave Seth a look of gratitude and relief as they passed each other. Seth then cantered away.

They all looked up as Seth's owl circled above them.

"Yes, he's seen where Lola is," said The Magician. He then looked down at Pixey. *"Don't worry little one."* She could usually understand much of what he sent, though not as clearly as when Lola sent. *"Lola is alright and the owl does not want you for his dinner."*

Seth cantered down the track and was back at the farmyard in just a few minutes.

"Sir!" he called as he saw Caitlin leading Lola's father to the house. "Sir," he said again as he got closer.

Lola's father turned. He looked at the breathless Seth. Seth's owl was now circling over the farmyard. Lola saw her father come back towards Seth. They were talking to each other. Seth put his hand on her father's shoulder. Her father nodded his head, reaching across to Seth's shoulder in a somewhat awkward but heartfelt embrace. Seth then got back on his horse and turned and rode back up the track. Her father was waving now, not seeming quite so defeated. Lola felt pleased. She watched him for a little longer. He did care for her. From this perspective, she could really see that he did care for her. There was now a feeling of delight and comfort deep inside her. She pulled back away from the sky. *"I'll find you again,"* she sent to the owl. Then she could feel the cold on her back from the damp draughty cell. She curled up into a little ball. She had always been loved, that was a reason to get home. She would find a way.

CHAPTER 12

Another Well

Oskar was back. He sat in front of the bars. *"I shall pretend you are not my girl. The men are around,"* he sent. *"They must not know."*

Lola sat up. Yes, that was a good plan. He was a clever dog. Lola kept her gaze down but sent, *"Have you remembered where you heard the keys?"* She hoped there was no one able to pick up their conversation.

"I am thinking 'keys', but my ears cannot remember yet," Oskar sent back. The keys meant Lola would be able to come out and play sticks. He would try to remember.

There were footsteps and shuffling. Then the rattle of keys. Oskar glanced at Lola, his ears pricking up.

"Any signs of life in this one?" a voice growled.

A man glanced into the cell. Lola was caught off guard and looked back.

"Aagh, not playing dead anymore, are we?" he continued in his gruff voice.

His clothes were greasy and worn like everything else in the prison. He had unkempt, black hair that fell to his shoulders, a thick beard and bushy eyebrows that disguised much of his features except for his hooked nose. His skin was pallid as if it had never seen the light of day. A stale rancid smell came from him, whisky or something similar and too much of it. Lola had only ever smelt whiskey when she was at the fair with her father. Once her brothers had some and it made her father very angry. He would never allow that kind of thing on the farm. He said it made men lazy and sometimes violent.

Lola heard metal clanking. She saw the guard had two beaten-up tin mugs in his hand. "I suppose you'll be wanting food then," he muttered and then disappeared out of sight. She heard him grumbling to someone else in the next cell. He reappeared and carelessly thudded one tin mug down in front of the cell. "Better drink it. It's all you'll get." The man disappeared back up the passage.

"Watered milk," Oskar sent. *"It's safe, they give it to me."*

Lola's stomach churned again, but this time from hunger. She picked up the mug. The contents looked like gray dirty water. She sipped it. She could just about drink it, her hunger overriding her taste buds. It was cow's milk, not something she was used to.

There was more shuffling. The man appeared again. He pushed a piece of bread through the bars and held it out to Lola. She looked at him. His eyes were dark and bloodshot. He had little to no focus. It was as if he was blind to what was before him, regardless of the suffering. Lola slowly reached out and took the bread. It was hard, but it was food.

The man growled and grumbled to himself as he

shuffled to the next cell and gave the other prisoner a piece of bread that he had in his other hand. He then shuffled and grumbled his way back down the passage. "Come dog," he snapped as he passed Oskar.

"It's my outside time," sent Oskar. *"Not real outside like with you in our minds. I will find those keys and then we can go outside for real. The man never goes outside. We can get away from him if we go outside."*

Lola watched Oskar follow the man. There was no sign of the spring in his step that she expected when a dog followed his master, especially a dog as young as Oskar. His tail was down and his ears were drooping.

Lola dipped the bread in the milk. It was a better way to have both. The bread settled well in her stomach. Whoever it was who had imprisoned her seemed to want to keep her alive. She just had to try to outsmart them. She had done this with the serpents once, but was it the serpents, she wondered, or someone stronger that she faced this time?

It was much later in the day that Lola heard movement from down the stone passage. It was the man again.

"You, up now." He was pointing at Lola. She just sat there and stared back.

"I said up!" bellowed the man.

Oskar was now beside him. Lola could feel Oskar's nervousness. He suddenly had divided loyalties, which he didn't quite understand, but this was not the time to show them.

Lola stood up. *"I think they want me alive for the*

moment. Pretend you don't notice me," she sent to Oskar, worried he might try to protect her.

The man came over and unlocked the cell door. Lola stood fast just a few feet away from the opened door. The man lunged towards her and tried to grab her arm. She pulled slightly out of his way and he stumbled, but quickly recovered himself.

"What is it that you want?" asked Lola in her bravest voice.

"I don't want anything," the man snarled. "I would have had you thrown back into the sea by now - but the Lord seems to think you are very important - that you can sort out his young misguided bard and oversized snakes."

"Well, then you had better take me to him, but I assure you I can walk without your assistance." Lola stepped around him and out of the cell. She couldn't believe how she was speaking to this wretched man. Yet, for some reason, she had a newfound confidence and felt very secure in herself. Was she still being guided by Eva's protection? Lola had no idea how she was going to escape, but she wasn't going to find that out by staying in her cell. She needed to know more about where she was and what was wanted from her.

Lola walked a little away from her cell but the man quickly caught up with her. He took her arm and she slapped his hand. "I will come with you on my own accord." She walked briskly past him.

Outside of her cell, she could see into the next one. There was the man with the dog. He had dark skin, soft brown eyes and high cheek bones. Though he was unshaven, she could see he had a kind face. His skin was weathered, as if he was the type of person who was happiest spending his time outdoors. She looked closer. His eyes, his eyes were the same as Morgan's were, the girl she had looked after on her father's farm. He watched her with a sense of worry in his gaze. Behind him, curled up in what seemed like a ball of grief and sadness, was a grey looking dog. She guessed it was the grey and white collie that Morgan had told her about.

The guard pushed Lola in the back, impatient with her hesitation. "Up the stairs!" he bellowed, trying to sound in control. He was disconcerted by Lola's boldness.

Lola made her way up a winding stone staircase. She could feel Oskar's uneasiness. As she embarked on the first step, she remembered him telling her that some people didn't come back when they went up there.

"Don't worry," she sent. *"I'll be back."*

"Yes, yes, you're my girl," she heard him send back nervously.

Once around the first corner, the stairway became very dim and narrow, lit only by a single torch on the wall. It was not a long staircase and soon they were in front of a dark wooden door with iron studs. The guard reached up to a hook to its side. Hanging there was a large bunch of keys. He took them and opened the door, pushed Lola through and closed it behind him, but did not lock it. He hung the second set of keys on his belt.

Lola found herself in a huge open hall. The floor was made of polished black marble. The windows down both sides let light in that threw a mirror-like sheen onto the floor. It was a cold light, as if the floor soaked up any warmth that might have been sent by the sun then threw back an icy glare.

In between the windows there were wall hangings depicting serpents of many kinds, mostly devouring human beings or animals. One was devouring a tree as it coiled around it. They were all black with gold borders and gold was the main thread used in their embroidery. Though they were exquisitely made, these did not impress Lola like the tapestries in the King's castle. They were made with evil and power in mind, not devotion and creativity. It was as if they were made under duress, each depicting something more horrible, with pain in every stitch.

At the end of the hall there was a set of steps up to a golden throne. The cushions on it were black velvet. There sat a man. This man Lola also recognised. This man was olive-skinned with dark curly hair that was cut short on the sides. He had fine delicate features. This man, Lola thought, must be Ariella's father.

He was not a big man. In fact, he probably was not much taller than Lola herself, but he was a man who took up a lot of space. He filled the throne room end of the hall with a sense of power and importance that few would be able to stand up to. Lola took a deep breath. She would have to be at her strongest.

This man, she thought, was loveless. The Magician's words again echoed in Lola's mind. "The two greatest human emotions are love and fear. Of the two of them love is stronger, but we never give it time - we give into fear." She thought of those she loved to boost her resilience.

To the right side of the throne there was a black marble well, made of the same marble as the floor. This part of the room was dark and Lola could see a green florescent mist drifting from the well. Next to it, on a small fold-up stool made of mahogany, sat a boy who was probably about the same age as Lola. He looked up at her with deep dark eyes that peered from under a wavy crop of black hair. He too was dark, but ashen-looking, as if he had never spent any time anywhere but in this hall.

"I'm sorry," he whispered sadly as he met Lola's eyes.

"Silence boy!" shouted the man on the throne.

Lola realised that she had left the guard behind her and had ventured across the hall of her own accord, drawn to both the boy and the well.

"Well …" The man was eying up Lola with a cynical sneer on his face. "You don't look much, but then you didn't sound much in Umir's story. Yet he does capture you perfectly."

Lola looked back at the boy. Was this Umir? And who was he? She looked beside him. There, in a pile, was a stack of parchments covered in writing.

"Did you write about me?" she asked Umir as kindly as she could.

The boy, Umir, nodded. "I didn't know you were real." He looked away, not wanting to face Lola.

"You shall address me!" the man demanded.

Lola nearly jumped and quickly looked back at the man on the throne. "What did the boy write about me?" Lola tried to keep her confident, carefree air that she had used with the guard, but it was much harder. This man would not be intimidated.

"Oh, he wrote a lot about you, but what I want to know is how much of it is true and how much of it is a story." The man had a conniving whine to his voice that made him unpleasant to listen to. "Did you banish the serpents to the underworld never to speak again?" He was now shouting at Lola and lifting himself out of his throne seat while shaking his fist at her.

"That depends," replied Lola, biding for time. She could not remember exactly what she had said. She knew that she had banished them from speaking and stealing language while they wanted to cause menace. "That depends," she repeated while trying to keep composed. "Which serpents are you speaking of?"

"Which serpents?" The man seemed to whine and growl at the same time. "There are only ever two serpents. Every other is a reflection of these two - the mother serpent and her offspring - the root and the potential. For a spell-binder you know very little."

Lola glanced at the boy, who now had a look of alarm in his eyes. Did the man and this boy know more about her powers than she did?

"If you want to know what is true and what is not in the boy's story then I will have to hear it," Lola said assertively.

The man turned to the boy behind him. "Umir!" he barked, "Give the girl your parchment."

"Oh, that will be of no use," Lola began, trying to sound polite. "I cannot read very well. No, Umir will have to read his story to me. I will help him circle all of the things that are true."

"Doesn't your magician teach you anything?" The man's voice was scathing and Lola could feel herself wanting to defend The Magician, but she held her nerve.

"Oh yes, he teaches me much, but reading is not something I'm very good at. I'm much better at talking…" Lola stopped herself. She guessed that he would already know that she could talk to animals of all kinds from Umir's writing, but Oskar, she wouldn't want him to take Oskar out of the dungeon and away from her. "…at talking to serpents."

"As you are feeling so clever, go over and talk to them now," the man ordered, pointing towards the large urn-like well that Umir sat near.

Lola turned slowly and went over to the well. The green florescent mist started to churn. "*Lola.*" She heard a hissing whisper. "*Lola, we are obeying you, but we miss you. Forgive us, let us go.*"

Lola looked up at the man.

"Well, what are they saying?" he questioned.

Lola wondered if the man truly wanted to know, or was playing some game. "They are entreating me to release them." It was as honest an answer as she could give. She tried to sound formal in her answer, hoping it would sound like she knew what she was doing.

"Well, then release them!" the man roared.

"I cannot release them until I am absolutely sure what it is they want. I am not sure if I can release them here or if I must go back to the Forest Castle to do so."

"You will release them on my terms! You will put them under my command." The man was now standing and pointing at Lola.

"What is your name?" Lola tried to say respectfully and quietly so as to contrast with the man's voice.

"I am the Serpent Lord, feared and obeyed by all who encounter me. That is all you need to know." The man's voice was now cold and calculated, but Lola could sense an underlying unease with her boldness.

"Did your mother not give you a name?" Lola could see the man being slightly unnerved by her question.

"I am not who I was when I was in the care of my mother," the Serpent Lord replied in a deep staccato voice.

"It will be very difficult for me to help you if I do not know your true name," Lola continued, having no idea why she was saying what she was saying.

"You shall not have my name, you shall speak to my serpents and you will learn to show respect for those more powerful than yourself."

The Serpent Lord's voice continued to be deep and threatening. Lola felt it pierce through her like an ice dagger.

"If you don't," he continued, "I will start to cut off the fingers of this boy one day at a time until he never writes again."

Lola shrugged; her instincts were telling her to appear not to care, instincts which felt a million miles away from her actual feelings of horror at the thought that Umir could be tortured in this way. "Well, if you are going to do that you had better let me hear his story first, just in case he hasn't finished it properly."

"Boy!" The Serpent Lord now turned towards Umir. "Start reading."

Lola walked over to the steps by the well. She sat down out of sight of the Serpent Lord. She gave Umir a brief but reassuring smile. He tried to give a shy smile back and then picked up his parchment and began to read.

CHAPTER 13

Arrival

There was just a dim glow of light left when Marcus led the party of travelers over the crest of the path and into the Middle Valley. Pixey was asleep, nestled in the sling that he had tied around him. She seemed to settle as they left the Western Valley, perhaps sensing some familiarity near her birthplace.

About a mile down into the Middle Valley they entered the great evergreen forest. Here they stopped for a brief rest. The forest was filled with holly, yew, pine and some very tall trees that Ariella had never encountered before. Wrapped in a blanket under one of these tall trees, she sat mesmerised.

"What are these trees?" she asked The Magician, who was sitting close by. His sadness was interrupted momentarily by her genuine interest.

"They are called *sequoias* in their native land," he answered. "When people of our land are sent out on quests to find and protect the wisdom of the world, they also collect seeds and plants to preserve them as well. Things don't always take, but these trees have."

Ariella looked up again. The trees seemed to reach higher than the mountains.

The Magician smiled at Ariella's wonder. "They are

only babies. They grow much taller and live as long as the yews. Here," he handed her a cone from the tree, "its seed, keep it, and then you can plant it one day."

Ariella took the cone. She turned it over and over in her hand and then looked up at the trees again. How could this small brown parcel of a cone grow into the magnificent trees that she gazed up at in the fading light?

Marcus's men were very efficient and experienced in the woods. In no time they had a small fire going and were brewing tea. Marcus sat down beside the fire. Pixey's little feet and front paws stretched out of both ends of his sling. She was becoming restless and wanted to get out. Marcus caught Eva's eye. She registered his worry about letting Pixey roam free in the dusk light.

"Not more than a few steps away from Marcus," Eva sent.

Pixey stopped still for a moment on hearing Eva's words.

"I've told her not to roam," Eva reassured Marcus.

Morgan watched as the tea brewed and the men started to pass out hot steaming mugs. It was strange smelling tea with a hint of lavender, but not unpleasant. She brought a mug over to Ariella who was still taking a good look at her sequoia cone in the dim light.

"Here." Morgan handed Ariella the mug.

Ariella looked up. "Oh, thanks." She was not quite sure if Morgan had brought the tea out of friendship or duty.

Morgan stayed standing by Ariella and looked around. She breathed in the wood smoke from the tiny fire. "I love this," she said to Ariella. "This is what my father and I used to do as we travelled. You, your horse and" …Morgan's voice cracked.

"Your dog." Ariella finished Morgan's sentence for her. "I'm sorry Morgan. I never meant for you to be separated from Sona. I never meant for Lola to be separated from her little cat if that part is my fault too. I'm learning a lot. Just these last few days. I had no idea how real people lived, or how brave and capable they are. My father would have me think that anyone other than himself or immediate family were useless nit-wits." Ariella looked down at her cone and then up again. "Morgan," Ariella continued, "You know Lola said that she loved rowan trees? That they seemed to be her tree… Do you have a tree that seems to be yours?"

Morgan was still reflecting on Ariella's comments about her father and thinking about her own father and Sona being at his mercy. "Tree," said Morgan. "Tree, well, my tree is probably cedar. I love the smell of the wood. That is what they are burning now - just a few dry sticks from that tree over there."

"Ah," returned Ariella. "That is a nice smell." She paused and let her fingers run over the cone again. "I think mine is this tree." She looked up again at the sequoia. It disappeared into what was now an inky sky. "The Magician calls it sequoia. These are only young, he says. I love the way they reach into the heavens, almost like they borrow space from the sky. All of my life seems to have been controlled by what is underground, my father with his serpents and dungeons."

"Time to move on."

The girls' conversation was interrupted by Seth collecting mugs and rallying everyone. They watched as one of the men lit a torch and then passed the flames on to three others while another man put out the fire which had brewed their tea.

Seth was now organising the horses and came over to help Morgan and Ariella onto theirs. There was much shuffling and moving around of people and bags as the party readied to go.

"Pixey." Marcus's voice could be heard above the bustle. "Eva, I can't see Pixey. I think she was spooked by all of the movement."

"*Where are you, little one?*" Eva tried to send out. But she was just met with confusion and fear with no clue as to where it was coming from.

Eva looked over at The Magician. He smiled. He beckoned Marcus to come closer. He approached with his torch. There was a loud meow. It made Morgan and Ariella jump. They turned towards the light of the torch.

"Oh no!" cried Ariella. "She's being eaten."

The light caught the glowing eyes of a fox with Pixey in its mouth. It was a small fox and it cautiously stepped towards Marcus. Then Aya the fox gently put Pixey down at Marcus's feet.

Marcus knelt down and scooped Pixey up. Aya

pawed his bent knee as if to greet him.

"Thank you, dear little friend. You have come a long way to escort us."

Eva sent Marcus's message for him. Aya turned, ready to lead them down the path, leaving Ariella and Morgan to stare in amazement.

Darkness had fully set in now, and in the woods it was even darker. It was a clear night, which meant that it was cold. Although riding kept their bodies warm, feet and hands started to feel the bite of the oncoming winter.

Morgan didn't mind. She was used to the bittersweet feelings one had in the woods at night in cold weather. It was worth the cold to catch glimpses of the layers of stars in the winter sky and hear the sounds of owls echoing through the trees. Yet she so wished that her father and Sona were with her on this adventure instead of being at the mercy of Ariella's father. She had begun to feel very comfortable in the land they were in. Would that she had been born and raised here. She couldn't remember her mother. She only knew that her father had cared for her since she was an infant. Though her mother lived, she was of a station in life that wouldn't have allowed her to have a daughter. Her father said that she was the most beautiful woman he had ever known.

Morgan never really felt she had missed out. Like Lola, she was glad for the freedom that a life in the woods and simplicity had given her. But she was old enough now to live on her own. Perhaps she should come and live here in this rich and abundant place rather than the rocky and arid land that she and her father had been living in over the last few years.

The journey ended at midnight. After they passed the guards and entered the castle walls, various knights, grooms and ladies came to greet them. Of course the King did too. For now, as it had always been before the serpents' enchantment, he met his guests on the castle steps with Lance by his side. He never made guests enter the throne room in a formal way.

The King warmly welcomed the girls. He himself helped them down off of their horses. "You have nothing to fear from us, Morgan and Ariella," he explained. "Ariella, I shall do whatever I can to resolve any dispute your father believes he has with us."

Ariella looked at the King uneasily, but he smiled kindly at her. "Of course, neither of you, shall be sent anywhere without it being your own wish. You are not bargaining tools for the return of Lola."

Then everyone was off to bed for a good rest with a promise to talk further in the morning.

The Magician went to his favourite room, Eva to a smaller room next door, and Ariella and Morgan to the ladies' quarters. They had this room to themselves. The 'ladies' who had populated it before had all returned to their former selves: squirrels, martins and even a badger. They had returned to their dwellings in the woods and fields. The beds were freshly made with the sheets impeccably ironed and their edges folded over warm wool blankets. The fire had been built up.

Both welcomed the warmth and snuggled down onto their freshly stuffed mattresses.

A small tortoise-shell cat suddenly appeared from behind the wardrobe. She jumped up and sniffed both of them, as if to be sure they had everything they needed.

"This must be Sophie," Ariella smiled. She did actually like cats although she had never been allowed to have one.

"Yes," replied Morgan sleepily.

Sophie jumped down and looked at the girls one more time. Then, satisfied that they were settled in, she disappeared into the corridor. She knew she had her own settling down to do with Pixey back in their bed at Milly's cottage.

CHAPTER 14

Bound

Lola was brought up from the dungeon for one hour a day to listen to Umir's story. She would sit on a step just below him by the serpents' well and listen to him weaving a tale about a twelve year old girl who was a magician's apprentice. This girl could talk to animals and had to find a way to conquer an evil enchantment. She had the assistance of two knights, one of whom had been turned into an owl.

All the time the Serpent Lord, with his back to the well, listened too. He always had something threatening to say to Lola to try to scare her. However, she began to notice how, as each day passed, he seemed less interested in her and more preoccupied with his maps and scrolls. Lola tried to glance over at them as she walked past his throne; she could see lots of lines and triangular shapes, but she had no idea what they meant.

It was the last day that Umir would read to Lola. He was just reading the part where the Forest Queen arrived at her Castle and the wolves attacked, when there was a great commotion from the other end of the hall. Another man, tall and thin with a bald head and hook nose, came swiftly across the cold marble hall.

He was shouting words in a language that Lola had never heard before and waving his arms.

The two men completely ignored Lola and Umir and carried on what sounded like a very heated debate.

"Who is he?" Lola whispered ever so quietly.

"His brother-in law, the General," Umir replied, his words near silent. "They are arguing over the maps."

"What's on the maps?" Lola asked.

"The Three Valleys," whispered Umir again. "They are arguing over whether they can get over the mountain pass to The Three Valleys in the winter."

"But I've…." Lola stopped. That was what the maps were of - where she lived. Her stomach felt as if a claw had grown up out of it only to clutch her insides and begin to squeeze.

The new man now walked towards Lola and Umir. He was still talking loudly. He looked at Lola and seemed to say something that was angry and directed towards her. He then walked back and continued his argument with the Serpent Lord.

Lola tried to swallow and find her voice. All the while, the green ether from the well slightly hissed. Lola was aware that the serpents were always present and that they seemed aroused by the argument that the Serpent Lord and his brother-in-law were having.

"What did I say to the serpents, Umir? What did I say to bind them back into the underworld?" Lola had finally found her voice again.

Umir looked back down at his parchment and began reading again. He continued to read about how the animals paired themselves up, how they slowly inched themselves around the well at the Forest Castle to create a bonding circle, one that the serpents could not break and escape from. He then stopped and looked at Lola. "You don't remember what you said?" he whispered.

Lola shook her head. Then they both stood up. The two men were still arguing. They were completely engrossed in the maps and scrolls pointing to different sections, pushing one part aside and then arguing over another.

Lola looked directly into Umir's dark eyes. He was perhaps a little younger than her, she was sure, but, as The Magician would say, he had a very old soul. She reached for his hand. Slowly they walked around the well. Their steps left a trail of golden light that warmed the corner of the room along with their cold bones and numb fingers.

Their bond was strong. Somehow Umir knew everything of Lola's life; somehow he had borne witness to everything she had done. Neither knew how, but it would mean that neither would ever feel quite as lonely again.

They stopped when they completed the circle. The well started to hiss and spit. The green iridescent mist seeped out, but not past the circle of light, which Lola and Umir were standing on.

"Stay still and don't let go of my hand," Lola said to Umir. The ring around the well lessened its intensity as they stopped, but still glowed. The green mist continued to bellow.

The argument between the Serpent Lord and the General had stopped. They were both now staring at Umir and Lola.

"She's going to do it, she will call them forth. She can't help herself!" the Serpent Lord exclaimed in English.

"Lola, we await you. We have missed you."

Lola could hear the serpents' voices coming from deep within the well. She looked around. No one else reacted. She was the only one who could hear them.

"Give us your voice."

The mists seethed out as Lola heard this. Then the head of one of the serpents appeared.

"Look!" The Serpent Lord was now extremely excited. "She has called them forth! They will now be in *my* power." The Serpent Lord rushed towards the urn.

Umir instinctively put out his arm to stop the Serpent Lord. "No," he warned. "Not on your own."

"They are my serpents. I have always gone to my well," said the Serpent Lord indignantly.

"Not when they are really here," Umir tried to explain. "You have only seen a reflection of them. These are different."

Lola was standing still, focused, holding Umir's hand and staring at the well. She was aware of the Serpent Lord, but far more aware of what was happening in the well. She knew she had contained the serpents before, and now she knew she had to try to transform them.

She also knew, regardless of the consequences, she had to do exactly the opposite of what the Serpent Lord wanted her to do. Lola spoke. "I bind you. I bind you to natural law. You must never steal language again in this world or others. Your voices will be used for only speaking the truth, for pursuing good. And you will take no other form than the ones you presently have." And then, as if the memory of the words came from the parchment still in Umir's one hand, through him and to Lola's memory, there emerged the word that named and bound the Serpents. *"Byah, Byah, Byah, and I am Abyah!"*

Lola sent the words that the Forest Queen had originally given her in a dream, the words that the Forest Queen had always chanted around her well to bind the serpents.

"No!" The Serpent Lord now flew towards the well. There was a flash of green light that struck the corner of the room like lightening. The green mist bellowed out voluminous smoke. There was a high pitched screech and then the Serpent Lord's body convulsed and fell in a heap, half in and half outside of the circle.

The General rushed over and pulled the body away from the urn and down the marble steps.

"Fool, you fool, now you will never lead your army!"

The General's voice had a strong and harsh accent. He leant over to listen to the Serpent Lord's chest, and put his hand in front of the Serpent Lord's mouth. "He lives, but not much," he said, not sounding in the least sympathetic. He looked over at Lola.

"You stupid girl, calling forth those lousy snakes. They are always his downfall. He thinks he can control them, but they control him." He snapped his fingers towards the other side of the hall. "Guards! Get a physician and take this girl and this boy away while I decide what to do with them."

"Umir has done nothing wrong, he's only stated the truth," Lola entreated, still standing on the circle. "You must let him go home, he's caused no harm."

"He has encouraged my brother-in-law to dabble with fire through his ridiculous stories - that is wrong enough. Guards, take them, take them now!"

The guards came towards Lola and Umir and grabbed them by their upper arms. They roughly escorted them across the great cold floor to the door that led to the cells. The guard with the keys grabbed one of the rings from his belt and opened the door. Lola quickly flicked her eyes back and forth between the two key-rings as thoroughly as she could. Yes, she thought, the two key-rings, the one held by the guard and the one hanging on the wall looked the same. Umir caught Lola's eyes, and quickly nodded, affirming Lola's deduction. They were now being ushered down into the cells. Lola was thrown into her cell and the bars slammed shut, but Umir was dragged past. Lola heard another set of cell bars slam next to her, although she couldn't see where Umir had been taken. As with the cell to the left of her, Umir's cell was at an angle so prisoners couldn't confer, or even see each other.

Oskar witnessed Lola's rough treatment. Lola had to send messages to him to keep him from reacting as she could feel his protective instinct towards her rising in anger at the guard.

"I'm unhurt. The Serpents are bound at this well too. Perhaps all of the others now," she sent. *"We will make a plan, but let the guard settle back to his post before we do anything."*

It took all of Oskar's will to just sit and pretend he was still an obedient prison dog. He watched his supposed master grumble and stomp around and then finally settle at his table which was situated within view of both sets of stairs, the one leading up to the hall and the one leading down to Oskar's outside area.

Lola and Umir both slid down the cell wall to sit on the floor, ignorant of their opposing positions on either side of the wall that separated them. Oskar crept over to Lola and put a paw through the bars.

"The boy is just there. Only the wall is between you," Oskar sent as he peeped around the corner of the grey stone column that obstructed Lola's view of Umir's cell.

"I have always been so grateful to be able to communicate with animals, but now I need to be able to communicate with a human and I can't." Lola sank her head into her hands.

Oskar gave a sympathetic whine and tried to stretch his paw closer. Lola put her hand down and touched it and then gently stroked it. Contact with Oskar had made her feel better before, perhaps it would help now. Why, she thought to herself, did she have these swings in emotions of feeling brave and in control and then hopeless? She was a budding magician; shouldn't she feel brave all of the time?

Lola looked up at Oskar. *"He might be able to talk to you like I do,"* she sent. *"He's very intuitive."*

Oskar sat up and gave a small wag of his tail and disappeared behind the column.

Umir was sitting like Lola with his head in his hands. He was being tossed in a storm of his own feelings about his master, who he both admired and loathed. His beloved scrolls had been scattered all over the hall and had probably now been discarded or burnt. He also felt deep remorse at being the reason Lola was captured and now being mistreated.

He hadn't believed that she was in real danger, as the Serpent Lord needed her, but now that his evil brother-in-law was in control, he knew that they were both in danger. He knew that the General wanted land, all that he could get his hands on. He had heard that The Three Valleys held priceless treasures in their hills. The absence of the Forest Queen meant that, for once, they were not protected, at least from the Eastern side. He would enslave the people of the valleys and destroy the woods and farmland to find the treasure. He had no appreciation of any of its beauty.

Oskar stood in front of Umir. He put on his happy dog face, wagged his tail and tried to send thoughts of friendliness to start with. Umir looked up. He wasn't very experienced with dogs. He half smiled at Oskar's pleasant expectant face, but nothing else came. He was too far away for Oskar to reach a paw towards him. Umir just looked at him for another moment or two and then looked back down and disappeared inside himself.

"Dog!" the guard shouted from his station. "Out time."

Oskar knew he should respond as he always did to the word 'out'. There would be food for him in the round walled 'outside' he was let into late each afternoon. He walked past Lola's cell. *"Nothing,"* he sent.

"Keep your connection with me as you go up. It may help me find a way out," Lola sent back and stood up as she watched him pass.

"Of course, you are my girl - I will show you where I go. Maybe you can come up and play sticks there."

Oskar trotted after the guard. He kept Lola in his mind knowing now that they could exchange experiences. His heart swirled with desire to have her join him, hoping that they could play sticks for real, but also feeling a sadness that she was locked in her cell and that really he was simply going to the outside space to eat and do his business. They would let him sniff around for a few minutes while they smoked their pipes, but no one would really pay any attention to him.

Lola watched Oskar make his way down a crumbling set of stone steps. A wooden door barred the way out of a stone arch. The guard held up his keys to a dim torch set in an iron mount on the wall. He found the key and pulled open the door. It scraped the stone floor and made Oskar's ears smart.

Light now flooded the corridor. The arch led out to a round courtyard that was scattered with dirt and sawdust. There was another man in the courtyard working at a tanning bench. His hair too was black and greasy and seemed to stick to his head and then fall to his shoulders. He made long slow movements with a scalpel-like knife across a hide that looked like it had belonged to a small goat. Lola shuddered at the thought of this. The man nodded at the guard and pointed to a bowl of scraps on the floor beside him. This was Oskar's dinner. It didn't look much more interesting or appetising than what she had been given.

Lola scanned the courtyard as best she could through Oskar's experience. There was a gate, a large arched gate with a huge iron lock on it. The guard's key-ring had one particularly large iron key.

CHAPTER 15

Reunion

Sophie had made her way through the dark alleys of the castle grounds and up to the roof over Milly's courtyard. She jumped down and pushed her way through the little flap that Seth had made for her in his mother's back door.

The candle on the table made a dim glow. Of course Sophie could see perfectly well in the dark, but Seth, Marcus and Milly could only just make out her now very slim form as she weaseled her way through their chair legs.

Pixey was still in Marcus's satchel, looking around. Lance was with the King and not in his usual place by the door, where Pixey remembered him always keeping watch, so she remained half hiding shyly in her satchel.

Sophie knew it wasn't allowed, but these were extraordinary circumstances. She jumped up on the table and went over to Pixey.

"Oh heavens!" exclaimed Milly. "You nearly made me jump out of my skin Missy."

Sophie now started washing Pixey's head.

"*Ma, Ma, Lance is gone. We have to find Lola,*" sent Pixey. She was now pulling herself out of the satchel towards Sophie, even though Sophie's washing was very rough. At least it was familiar. Sophie continued to wash Pixey all over and then stopped, looked at her, and batted her over the head.

"You have to pull yourself together, young lady," Sophie hissed. She then chased Pixey off the table towards the food dish that Milly had prepared but Pixey had left untouched.

"And don't ever turn up your nose at Milly's food. You've no idea where the next meal is coming from. You'll be no good to Lola half-starved and sorry for yourself."

Sophie was now pacing around Pixey, making sure she ate every morsel. Marcus, Seth and Milly looked on, not quite knowing what to do or what to think.

Pixey finished the food and Sophie washed her again. *"I do love Coal, but oh, he does smell like a horse. I've only just got that smell out of my own fur and now I'll have to sleep with it again with you."*

"You will sleep with me on Lola's old bed?" asked Pixey as she sat obediently.

"Of course, if we are going to find Lola we have to put our heads together," replied Sophie. Sophie was now purring, as was Pixey.

"I think they are happy with each other again," Seth said. "They seem to be settling down."

So everyone in the castle grounds slept for the night, except Seth's owl. He flew overhead. He knew where Lola was. He knew the evil feel of it. He tried to send to Sophie in her sleep. She dreamt of musty smells, a growling dog and bitter cold, but with Pixey beside her she also dreamt of Lola's breath and her beating heart. She could not penetrate the distance though and connect with Lola's mind any further than knowing she was alive.

CHAPTER 16

A Ring of Keys

Oskar ate, did his business and sniffed around the barren courtyard. Nothing really interested him there, but he didn't know what Lola would see as important so he tried to sniff and notice everything.

"Dog, come." The guard had finished smoking his pipe.

The tanner stood up. "Wait," he mumbled and waved his hand towards the guard. He pulled out a sizable brown ceramic bottle from under the bench beside him. "Here." He handed it to the guard. "Come today with the General."

"Hump," the guard grunted. "Suppose there'll be more where that came from if things go his way." The guard took the bottle. "Dog," he snapped. Oskar followed him and they made their way back up the steps.

A few moments later Oskar was in front of Lola's cell again.

"Did you see where I was?" he sent.

Oskar was now alert and eager. Helping Lola had given him a sense of purpose in his life. Lola was still sitting against the wall where he had left her. Her eyes were closed. She slowly looked up and then opened her eyes. There sat her friend. His dark, loving eyes wanting to know what he could do next, and his blonde roughly cut coat fluffed around them.

"What was in the bottle?" Lola sent.

"Bad smelling water. Makes the guard dizzy and sweat and fall asleep. He'll forget food in the morning. Won't wake up until it passes. Falls over and is always angry after he drinks it. Don't know why he drinks it."

Lola could hear the guard banging around the tin cups. Someone came down the stairs. The guard growled and then acquiesced towards whoever it was. He then appeared with three sets of bread and thin broth. He shoved the food at each cell and a portion was taken at each turn. For once the bread was almost fresh.

Lola ate quickly, as did the other two. Over the past few days she had managed to find out more about the man in the next cell through Sona. He had been ready to set off to find Morgan when news came that both girls had been found and were safe and being cared for. The result of this message was that he had been immediately thrown into the cells for no apparent reason, but he was still being considered as a leader of a trek over the mountains. Sona was very sure that his boat was ready to sail and that it was docked out of the way so as not to be noticed.

Lola was thinking of all of these things as she ate. She had given up tasting what she was fed. She trusted that Oskar would be able to smell something that would be bad for her.

As she finished, she discretely put her hand out to stroke Oskar's head. *"Let me know when he becomes sleepy and stupid, when he won't notice if I talk to the others."* Lola scratched Oskar under the chin. *"You are a good dog. We'll get out of here, we'll be free."*

Oskar's heart raced with excitement at this suggestion, but he kept himself still.

The minimal heat of the day had now left Lola's cell and as the night grew on, the cold and damp increased. The only light came from a smoky torch on the wall across from the cells. Lola sat and waited. She tried to tune into Sona. *"If we got out, could you and the man lead us down to his boat and go?"* Lola had to send this message a number of times. Sona was so sad that it was hard to penetrate through her grief.

Lola wondered about how Pixey was feeling. She had made no attempts to contact Pixey or Eva. The cells were oppressive. She couldn't penetrate the stone walls to reach them with her mind. She had only had brief flashes of Seth's owl, which seemed odd to her. She had no idea it was the owl who had dropped the message telling of Morgan and Ariella's safety.

The guard continued to bang around out of sight of the cells. He laughed to himself and roared and threw something at the wall. Lola could pick up a faint smell of that drink her father had forbidden her brothers to consume at the fair. Boblin, though, had snuck a taste of it, before insisting that she give him some of her mint ice to cover the smell of his breath. It had done no good, he was found out anyway.

The smell filtered towards the cells as the guard chuckled to himself and sang. Oskar, pretending to patrol, walked past and sent, *"He's drunk almost all of it now. He won't notice anything."*

Lola took a deep breath before throwing caution aside. "Umir," she said out loud, "the keys, the keys at the top of the stairs, will they open everything?"

"Yes." It was as if Umir had been waiting for Lola to make the first move.

"What keys?" The man's voice came from the cell on the other side.

Lola directed her voice back towards him. "I think we can get the keys to escape, but we need to know we can be away fast. Is it true your boat is ready?"

"How did you know?"

"Sona told me. Can we go tonight if we can get the keys? Is there room for all of us?"

"It is a small boat, big enough for me and my daughter and the dog of course."

"We would not be much more than that. If we leave anyone behind they will be in grave danger," Lola stressed.

"How can you know this?" The man's voice sounded both fascinated and worried.

"I can talk to animals. It may not be common here, but where I live, where your daughter is, where they sent the message from, some people can do it."

"And this is a good time too," Umir's voice could be heard. "The General doesn't know Lola can do this

- The Serpent Lord does. If we go while he is still unconscious then it will take ages for them to figure out what has happened."

The guard was suddenly silent. They stopped, holding their breath. There was a crash.

"Oh, almost gone!" the guard bellowed. There was another crash and then he broke into song again.

"*He will be sleeping soon. The bad water is all gone,*" Oskar sent.

"Both of you," Umir called to them whispering as loud as he dared. "Make it look like you are sleeping in the far corner of your cell with whatever you have to pile up and then cover it with your sheep-skin. He won't notice until mid-morning when he comes to."

"Okay - don't say any more until we have the keys," Lola said. They were then silent and waited.

The guard sang his tuneless song many times into the night. Oskar paced, going back to Lola to reassure both her and himself until he finally came and sent, "*Now in a dark sleep. No waking until the bad smelling water pees out later.*"

Lola had to almost giggle at Oskar's interpretation of the guard emerging from drunkenness.

"*Oskar,*" Lola now sent. "*You must be very brave now. You must go up those stairs. Don't worry, you can come back down again and you won't have to see anyone. At the top of those stairs, by the light, is a hook. On the hook are the keys that you told me about. Stretch up and take them. The ring is a good size for you to be able to take in your mouth. Come back down with care so you don't*" *shake them about too much."*

"Stairs - they are not good stairs," Oskar sent back, looking at the steps with caution. *"But you are my girl and we will play sticks."* Oskar mustered up his bravest of hearts and carefully plodded up each stair. Lola stayed with him in her mind, sending him all the courage she could.

He reached the top quickly and looked around. Yes, he saw the hook by the torch. He pushed up onto his back legs to land his front paws on the wall either side of the hook. Then he carefully lifted the key ring off, holding it in his jaw. The hard part was now letting go of the wall without the keys jingling. He did it quickly hoping that it would only make a quick noise.

Lola winced at the sound of the keys echoing against the stone walls. Both Umir and the man were alerted. Sona was already focused and aware of Oskar's mission. The guard however seemed undisturbed by the sound.

Oskar gently made his way down the stairs. He tried to move slowly, but his pride in his accomplishment started to make his tail wag as he came towards Lola's cell.

"Sh-sh," Lola tried to send, but she had the keys dropped straight into her hands and clasped them together to stop the sound. Lola found her cell key, unlocked it and went straight to Umir who took the keys from her.

"I know these keys," he said as he quickly identified the one for his cell. "I know which goes to the different doors and gates." He unlocked his cell and then made for the cell with Sona and the man in it and opened their cell.

Sona and the man quickly came out of their cell. The man clasped Lola's and then Umir's hands. "I'm Henry," he said, "Let's go." Henry also seemed to know where he was going, so Lola followed.

Umir turned back. He swiftly went to each cell and locked it again. "We'll keep them guessing."

They all went around the bend in the corridor. They had to carefully negotiate the broken ceramic jugs and tin cups on the floor. Oskar's excitement was barely containable as they made their way to the courtyard. Lola was taken aback by the filth and the stench. No one had ever cleaned up after poor Oskar.

Umir led them to the gate. He opened the lock with the correct key. "You first." He ushered Henry with Sona through. "Go Lola." Lola went through leaving enough space for Umir and Oskar to follow.

Then there was a clank of metal. Lola turned around. Umir and Oskar stood on the other side of the gate. Lola could see Oskar's loving and expectant eyes confused by the bars that now separated them. Umir locked the gate.

"Go Lola, if the dog is gone they'll find you even quicker. I'll be safe. They'll use me to find you. He won't dare harm me if he needs me to find you."

"But Oskar, I promised him." Lola turned forward to see Henry standing in both disbelief and frustration.

"Remember, I know your life. You must do

everything your magician says and leave thoughts of us behind, this is the only way. Tell the dog we are playing a game again."

"I can't lie, he will know."

"But he'll do what you say - you have no choice. Go!"

Lola's heart seared with distress at the sight of the trusting Oskar sitting on the other side of the gate. "Go with Umir, just for now. We will play sticks soon."

Henry sensed Lola's hesitation and grabbed her by the arm.

"Come now!" He pulled her across the track into the barren landscape. The silver of the moon was setting on the horizon. It was further into the night than Lola had realised.

"You must run, you can't stop. Neither the night or the tide will wait," Henry panted as he continued to pull Lola along. He had been as inactive as Lola over the last week and now running was hard on their stiff cold limbs.

Umir gently led Oskar back down the stairs. "It's okay dog, we'll play the game again". They carefully picked their way through the broken ceramics and tin cups. The guard was still snoring and muttering to himself, drenched in the smell of whiskey.

Umir went over to his cell, opened it, went in and locked it. They would use him to find Lola. He knew this. He would write about her whereabouts, not being able to write anything but the truth. Yet he knew if she got back to The Three Valleys she would be as safe as she could be. He didn't know what would happen to Oskar who now sat in front of him expectantly, not understanding that the night's happenings were now over.

Umir handed the keys back to Oskar. He pointed up the stairs. "Put them back," he said softly, trying to sound encouraging.

Oskar picked up the keys. He walked over to the stairs. He put them down. He looked over at Lola's cell. He looked up the stairs. No Lola, no hope, no sticks. These keys were hope and now she was gone. He went over to her cell. Sniffed. There had been Lola - there had been his girl. Now she was gone and his hope of playing sticks and of having his own person had been taken. Suddenly he understood every ounce of sadness that Sona had been feeling, but he wasn't going to let it make him crumble like it had her. No, he would howl it out. Everyone would know his brave heart was breaking. He would howl until the stone walls around him crumbled.

Umir had to cover his ears at the sound that came from Oskar. Even the guard was shaken out of his drunken state and started stumbling around and swearing, checking the cells. The guard shone his light into Umir's and nodded. He then tried to make out what was sleeping at the back of Lola's cell.

Oskar continued to howl. Lola could both hear and feel Oskar's distress.

"Don't stop!" shouted Henry. "You won't live to see that dog again if they catch you."

Sona was shooting ahead. Light was now revealing a sparkling line on the horizon. The sea - the way Lola had come here, though she remembered nothing of the journey.

In the distance Lola could hear men, dogs and horses. Still Oskar's howl was clear amongst them. He would be safe at least. He would be praised for raising the alarm. It would be the guard who would have the explaining to do.

In between the howls, Lola could hear Oskar sending, *"My girl, I am coming, you are my girl!"*

Lola now started willing him to run faster, to get ahead and to escape with them. She tried to slow slightly, but Henry pulled her along. They were now on sand and then they were going over wooden planks that had been built on the beach.

"Not far," Henry panted. "As long as she's been left alone, she's ready to go." Henry quickly led Lola down a series of planks and docks. They came to a small boat covered with a tarpaulin. Henry pulled it back. "Yes!" he exclaimed as if in victory, "we're off."

Lola stood frozen on the dockside. Sona was already in the boat. Oskar's howling was closer, as was the barking of the other dogs and the shouting of the men.

Henry pulled Lola into the boat, untied the securing lines and pushed off just as Oskar's face appeared on the dock's edge. Oskar stopped. He had never been in deep water before.

"Jump Oskar!" Lola shouted out loud, willing him

towards her.

He couldn't. He had never jumped into water and swam this way before. He paced the dock whining. Henry was raising the main sail and the wind was catching it.

"Jump Oskar, swim," Lola sent.

Oskar didn't understand swim. He had spent too much of his life in the darkness of the cells. Lola turned to Henry.

"Sorry," Henry said, sliding over to the tiller and pointing the boat into the southwest wind to catch the outward tide.

"Sona, tell him!" Lola sent and then realised Sona was already trying to explain, but Oskar couldn't bring himself to leap into the water and the boat was getting further away. Away from the now arriving men. Away from Oskar.

"Stupid mongrel!" The guard had a short whip, which he now struck Oskar with. It smarted across his back. Lola both felt and saw this.

"Run!" sent Lola, *"run away!"*

Oskar now remembered what his mother said. Before humans make you bad, you must run away and find good ones. Don't ever let a human make you bad.

Now Lola could hear Sona sending too. *"Run, run up through the cold white rocks. It's very cold, but there is a way to your girl. The wolves will help. I have seen this in my man. He has gone this way. The wolves know Lola - keep thinking of her - the wolves will help you then. They are like us but have no people. Run now, faster than you ever have."*

Oskar reached to the bottom of his heart for a second time and turned. He growled at the guard and then crashed through the dogs and the other men and horses and followed what Sona was willing him to do. Up, up with sharp sticks falling around him. He kept running and they missed him.

He ran until the ground was cold and slippery and the voices distant. He slowed, but then he heard Sona's voice again. *"Run, run until you can only hear the wind."*

Sona looked at Lola. *"He is clear of the men. They won't go up that far. Not for a dog they presume will return when he is hungry."*

"Will he be alright? Is there a way over?" Lola sent back.

"Ask my man," returned Sona who now looked out to sea.

Lola turned to Henry. "Is there a way over the mountains?"

"In the summer, yes. I have gone many times. It leads to the Forest Castle. But this time of year the snow is already deep on the tops. I don't know." Henry was focusing on the boat and wind and the outward sea.

Lola looked back. The land was far now, but she could still see the men shouting and making a drama on the docks, though no one had got into a boat yet. Then Lola looked up at the mountains. The ones that shielded her land from this desolate one. The mountains were higher than she imagined. How Oskar would get over she didn't know. At least he was free.

"Don't go back," she tried to send. She could still feel a slight echo of him sending *"Lola, my girl."*

Lola turned her gaze away from the mountains and towards the sea. "How do you know about the Forest Castle?" she asked Henry.

"The Forest Queen was my friend before she was taken by the serpents. There was even talk of a maiden from this land being presented to your King through her. But the serpents confused this and then, as you know, took her over. I stayed away, not wanting harm to come to my daughter. I thought we were safe just serving the Serpent Lord in a discreet way, that we wouldn't really be noticed. How wrong I was. Umir's tale revealed everything. The Serpent Lord saw me as a guide who could help him across the mountains to seize the Forest Castle and the serpents' well before a new Forest Queen could be established. He thought he could use *you* as his puppet."

"Me? He actually thought he could take over the Forest Castle through me?"

Henry's focus was now on the open sea. The waves had heightened and the wind had quickened. "Yes, you," he returned in a distracted way. "Don't underestimate him or his brother-in-law, the General. This is not over yet."

Henry then pushed a wooden box towards Lola with his foot while steadying the boat with the tiller. "Open it. There is water and some crisp bread inside. Have some and get some down Sona. We are in for a rough voyage. We are already dehydrated to start with.

You may bring it up again, but it will have some effect."

Lola obeyed even though she was already feeling queasy. Henry tacked the boat westward. For Lola this was the direction of home.

CHAPTER 17

Plans

Lola had been missing for five days. In that time, plans and decisions had been made at the castle about their best course of action. The King assembled a party of soldiers on the beach with Lars in charge of three ships to take to the Serpent Lord's lands if the word was sent to do so. The weather was a constant obstacle and the King and The Magician warned against any action without the knowledge that a clear run of weather was guaranteed. At this time of year that was nearly impossible. They did not know whether the Forest Queen still had influence over the weather that protected the headland of the Eastern Valley, or the weather was just following its winter patterns, but the sea was no place of safety. Eva and Seth's owl circled the cliff around the Middle and Eastern valleys. No day presented any opportunity to travel by sea.

"She is still alive and relatively unharmed from what I can tell," reported The Magician when they discussed the urgency of the matter in an early morning meeting the first day of their arrival at the castle. He spoke from the brief snippets Seth's owl was able to give him and from his own intuition.

"I know I would be able to tell much more from the Forest Castle," said Eva. If you can manage without me patrolling then I suggest you let me make my way there. The serpents could even be of use to us."

"It's been four days now," said the King. "With the snow falling as it is now it will take at least another day to get there. Will you know straight away what to do once you arrive?"

Eva and The Magician looked at each other. Calling up the serpents without a Forest Queen to give them stability was very risky, but trying to rescue Lola from the Middle Valley by boat or over the mountains would probably mean that other lives would be risked or even lost. Whose life was more valuable?

"We may be able to get the serpents to help us communicate with Lola," explained The Magician. "They are bound to her. They may be bound to her safety. We may be able to reach her mind through them so no one around her knows that she is communicating with us."

"So you both can communicate with the serpents and with animals?" asked the King.

Eva and The Magician looked at each other again. The Magician then looked down at his hands, which he was folding and unfolding. If only being a magician meant that he could weave a spell, the enemy would be conquered, Lola safe again and all would be well. No, being a magician meant having a bit more intuition than the average person, a bit more wisdom and understanding and the ability to constantly let go to welcome the new into life's processes.

He looked up at the King. "The truth is - we have no idea. Never has anyone but the Forest Queen been able to calm the serpents. Never has there been anyone who can connect and communicate with our friends in other species so reliably, and never has there been such a young person in my care who could reach out beyond her mind as Lola can. Usually it takes years of training. Lola can just do it. I do not think that the Serpent Lord will physically harm her. Somehow he has found out how powerful she is. She is far too valuable to harm. What I am worried about is what he might be able to do with the serpents unleashed on his side of the mountains. When Lola bound them to her she had no experience of the outside world. As you know, we are just one reflection of it. A very important one, but isolated in many ways. She had no inkling that there was anywhere but these three valleys. She has no understanding that this is only a small part of the world. She may be gifted, but she is young. Youth can often be misled when threatened."

The King sat back from the long oak table that they were seated around. He folded his arms across his chest. Lance quietly whined as he processed the King's thoughts over what The Magician had just said.

"So you both need to go to the Forest Castle," the King said after a moment's thought.

"No," said Eva, "not just us. We need to go with as many people as possible who are close to Lola, save Milly. Like Lola's father, Milly in her everyday routine will be a stronger pull than she would be if she came with us. But Marcus, Seth, the owls, Lance and you must all come."

"But who will keep guard here?" asked the King. A return journey to the Forest Castle was not exactly a return journey he wanted to make.

"It will be different, Lola will sense me," Lance sent to the King. *"The Forest Queen is gone."*

"I think we also need to bring Pixey," Eva continued. "She can send her thoughts to Lola over long distances. If she is not part of this then Lola's connection with her might not be as effective when their training starts properly. Our danger is from uncontrolled serpent wells at this point more than it is from the sea or the mountains."

"That's settled then," the King agreed. "We shall go as soon as horses and provisions are ready, even if we have to journey through the night."

While this meeting was happening Sophie was holding her own with Pixey. *"You were not sent to be Lola's companion to just spend your life having fun and games. Not that there is anything wrong with chasing butterflies or broom bristles when the time is appropriate. But your person is in danger and that is when you must take life much more seriously and push yourself. We are going to the castle now to offer your help in whatever way is necessary. We are going to the castle up over the roof tops."* Sophie then turned and promptly disappeared through her little door at the back of the cottage.

"Ma," Pixey both sent and meowed. *"I'm still small."*

"You are not nearly as small as you were when you were born," Sophie sent back. *"Now push your nose through that door and follow me. Both your brother and sister do this now."*

"Humph," thought Pixey. *"I won't be outdone by Little One. Then he would take all of the food because he was better than me."*

Pixey pushed the small door with all her might but it barely budged. Sophie waited patiently on the other side, but was silent so as not to give a hint that she might be there to help. Pixey backed up and ran towards the door. Her weight at running pace opened it and she tumbled through, but it swung back and pinched the end of her tail, which made her jump and crash into a flower pot.

"Ouch!" Pixey got up and shook herself off and then quickly washed the smarting end of her tail.

"Lesson one," sent Sophie. *"Always put one leg through and lever with your nose. Do it slowly, keeping the tail as close as possible to the body."* Sophie then turned and jumped up on the table at the back of the courtyard.

Pixey looked at her mother disdainfully. Then she saw claw marks on the leg of the table. The others would have used the table legs to climb up. Pixey jumped onto the table leg and hung on. She would have been scolded if she had done this on the table in The Magician's cottage, but this table was outside so maybe, she thought, it was different. She started inching her way up to the top. There were nobbly carvings at the top of the table leg. She used these to push off with her back legs and pull herself up to the same level as Sophie.

"Good, now for the flower pots." Sophie jumped onto a flower pot built into the wall. There was a series of them making steps up to the roof, if you were a cat of course.

"Be careful of the flowers. Milly loves these particular flowers," chimed Sophie as she delicately negotiated each pot without disturbing a single stem.

To Pixey these pots were miles apart, rather than just a short hop. She readied herself to spring two or three times before she had the courage to do it. She reached out her front paws to grab the edge of the first pot but found her legs dangling in the air without anything to push off of to bring her all the way up.

"Curl into the pot." Sophie was now on the roof edge. Even if she wanted to, she knew Pixey was now too big to be carried up by the scruff of the neck. Primo and Bella had done this with little trouble after a few goes. Surely Pixey could too, she thought.

Pixey curled her feet under and scrambled up the side of the pot. This helped her pull herself onto it, although the request to be careful of Milly's flowers was completely ignored. Pixey used one stem between her teeth to steady herself. The next three pots were much closer and Pixey managed these with less drama.

Sophie was now standing on the ridge of the roof. *"You have to jump and then almost run up the tiles. Think forward or you will slip back."*

Again Pixey readied herself amongst Milly's

withering dahlias, which were planted high to keep them from being eaten by snails. She pushed off and stretched her body with all of her might - just thinking forward. Her paws made contact with the slate. It was slippery like ice and cold in the early morning on the pads of her feet. Pixey's instinct was to lift her paws off the slates because of the unpleasant experience, but Sophie kept sending, *"Forward, up, up!"*

So Pixey willed herself forward and up, curling herself inward to find something to push her back feet off of. After what seemed like an eternity of scraping and scrambling, she was on the crest of the roof with Sophie.

"Good, you did that the first time. It took your brother and sister about three goes to do it without falling back into the pots. Milly has only just re-potted that last one."

Pixey shook herself off, feeling only a little proud, but mostly in awe of how high they were.

The roof had a slight groove in its crest and this was easily wide enough for an agile cat to make her way along. Sophie seemed to glide down the centre of the roof. Pixey's balance wasn't quite as sound and wobbled. She found that she was better if she just looked at the roof in front of her and not the view.

The roof backed onto a whole row of cottages and then came to a window in one of the upper stories of the castle. This was often left open for Sophie now, unless there was a fire lit. The fire being lit usually meant that there was someone sitting by it and Sophie would simply paw at the window to be let in.

This time Ariella and Morgan were sitting by the fire. They had been looked after mostly by Milly, who found them some soft wool pinafores and slippers to put over their cotton gowns. The clothing was some of the finest that women at the castle wore, but of a very simple design. Both were happy in their attire, neither wanted to be dressed like a princess by the Serpent Lord's standards.

It was Morgan who went to the window. "Look, two cats, well one's a kitten. Oh, Pixey!" Morgan exclaimed as Pixey proudly followed Sophie onto the windowsill.

Sophie jumped past Morgan. She squeaked and Pixey followed. *"Say hello and then follow me. It's always important to let humans know you have noticed them,"* Sophie instructed.

Both cats made a respectful fuss of the girls and then scampered off down the corridor.

The King was just standing up from the table where the meeting to discuss their next plan of action had taken place. Lance gave out a slight whine.

"Ah, we have visitors." The King smiled at Eva and The Magician.

Eva went over to the door and opened it before Sophie had a chance to scratch it to announce herself. Lance came over, very excited at the sight of Pixey who he had not really seen the night before, as she had been hiding in her satchel. He did manage to keep himself in check so as not to overwhelm her. He went over and gently wagged his tail and sniffed her. Pixey began to purr and rub up against his legs.

"*Lance,*" purred Pixey, "*I'm brave now. Ma says that's the only way. We shall go together to get Lola. You will know where to find her.*"

The King reached down and picked up the purring Pixey. She was a little surprised by this, but kept purring.

"We shall do our best, Little Three," he said out loud, "with your help of course."

Sophie looked around, then she sent to The Magician, "*There, you have her now and make sure no one babies her. It's time for her to grow up.*"

The Magician leant down and scratched Sophie under the chin. "*We'll do our best, little friend,*" he promised.

CHAPTER 18

Rescue

Munching on the crisp bread settled Lola's stomach a little. Sona happily ate some and lapped water. Sona seemed in better spirits now that she was in the boat and away from the prison, even though falling out would mean drowning in the rough sea. She was with her man and doing what he did. She had a sense of purpose again.

Henry was sailing the boat southwestward. He knew he had to sail away from the cliffs before he could tack back into the land in the Middle Valley. That is if they could reach the Middle Valley. As the strong winds took them out, there appeared dark clouds billowing over the western horizon.

"Snow," Henry said matter-of-factly. "Curl up with Sona as much as possible. Tie yourselves in with that line. You will need to keep each other warm. Hopefully the wet won't kill you." Henry knew that the hours ahead would run the danger of both being blown too far out to sea and hypothermia. He would keep moving, that would help, but Lola was slight and would easily freeze to death.

Lola snuggled down as tightly as she could next to Sona in the bow of the boat. Sona understood the importance of staying warm. Lola pulled some of the tarpaulin over them. That made a difference. At least much of the water ran off and only their feet were really wet.

Now Lola did something she hadn't dared to do the whole time she had been in the Serpent Lord's dungeons. She tried to send to those she loved in The Three Valleys. She couldn't decide to whom, but as had happened before, Seth's owl came into her mind. *"We are coming, we have escaped. We are coming by sea."* This was all she could do before the sea became too perilous.

Waves splashed over the bow, soaking most everything now. Henry was a skilled sailor but he couldn't control the roughness of the sea. They kept their southwest course until they could see the end of the mountain range that separated The Three Valleys from the Serpent Lord's kingdom. Even though it was nearing winter, Lola was struck by how green it suddenly looked after the arid landscape they had left. Her heart started to race. Although it was miles away, she could see it. She could see her home.

Henry, however, looked grim. The waves were quickening and each one went over the boat now, sometimes breaking on top of them. Lola and Sona were keeping warm under the tarpaulin but both were now completely soaked. The little boat was taking on too much water to last much longer. As Henry looked across to the west he could only just make out the ridge of hills that separated the Eastern Valley from the

Middle Valley, and between them and that ridge the storm was beginning to rage.

"We've no chance," he shouted through the roaring wind. "We can go out and try to go around it or we can go back. Do you want to fight the storm or the Serpent Lord?"

Going back, thought Lola, maybe this would mean finding Oskar, but she had told him to run away and, from the bottom of her heart, that was what she hoped he had done. Going out and then to the Western Valley, that would take a long time. There was no guarantee that they would make it. Lola could see the gravity of the situation in Henry's face.

"What to do?" Lola asked and tried to focus deep within herself.

"*Lola,*" a slightly high-pitched version of Eva's voice called in Lola's mind. "*The seas are too high. You must come into the cliffs.*"

"*Lola,*" the voice was familiar, it was Seth's owl. "*Lola, they will help you up the cliff. There is no other way. The storm is too strong.*"

Lola squinted her eyes and tried to shield them from the constant spray flying in her face. Suddenly everyone was flooding into her consciousness: The Magician, Eva, and Lance. She could feel the pull towards the cliffs from them all.

"*This way!*" It was Eva's voice again.

Lola could see two birds circling above the cliffs that guarded the Eastern Valley. It was a seagull and an eagle owl.

"*Tack now before it is too late. Marcus is here with ropes,*" sent Seth's owl.

"*How did you know?*" Lola said quietly in her mind to Seth's owl.

"*I have been following you even though you have shut us out and Eva has spoken to the serpents. Hurry!*" Seth's owl came out a little further to reassure, but went back in quickly so as not to risk the raging wind.

Lola turned to Henry. "We must go in to the cliffs. They are there with ropes for us."

"You must be mad, there is no way up."

"I know. I know they will be there!" Lola entreated Henry.

"The boat will smash into the cliffs before we can get onto dry land!" Henry shouted back.

"*He won't do it,*" Lola sent. "*He says the boat will smash on the cliffs.*"

"*There is one safe way,*" sent Eva, "*meant to fool sailors, but we can rescue you from the ledge once you climb.*"

"What about Sona?" Lola sent back.

"*You will have to tie her to one of you, otherwise she won't make the climb,*" Eva replied. "*Tell Henry that a seagull and an eagle owl will guide you in. He will have to believe you if we appear. We are coming now.*"

"Please!" Lola cried, begging Henry. "They will guide us in. They knew we were coming. I really can talk to animals. They wouldn't say to do this if it wouldn't work."

Henry still looked skeptical, but the western wind was battering them now. At least it would be slightly calmer for a short time if they tacked back in. He looked at the horizon of the Eastern Valley and there, sure enough, was a seagull and a large dark bird circling over sailor's folly. It was possible to get out onto the ledge and climb up, but the climb finished half way up the cliff with no hope of going up or down. Meanwhile the small cove that seemed protected would swallow up your boat from the current below.

"They will talk us in?" he shouted over the wind.

"Yes!" Lola's heart quickened with hope.

"Ready about!" Henry tacked in, leaning the boat into the wind. They suddenly were being pushed at a speed twice as fast as before.

Seth's owl called out in recognition of what they were doing. He flew out to meet them, soaring on his steady, powerful wings. Eva meanwhile, as a seagull, swooped and circled around the cliff.

"*Come back in now,*" Seth's owl sent. Lola translated. Henry tacked back again. The waves were getting bigger now.

"*Keep it steady,*" Eva sent. "*You will come to the break soon.*"

Lola could now see a ledge with a person standing on it. There was no seagull. It was Eva waving her arms. To Lola's amazement, she realised that Eva hadn't sent the seagull, she *was* the seagull.

Henry could also see Eva on the ledge and was relieved that this foolhardy solution to their plight might actually bear fruit. He kept the boat steady, hugging the tiller to keep her on course. "My last moments with you, old lady," he whispered to his boat. He knew she would be swallowed up.

It was another few minutes before the boat broke through a wave into calm slightly swirling water.

"Get her over here!" Eva shouted, reaching towards them.

Even though there was relative calm there was still a rocky scramble to get onto Eva's ledge.

Seth's owl flew past them. *"Well done, you!"* he screeched, and then disappeared over the cliff.

Lola immediately reached for Sona. Sona was a small collie, but Lola was still a small girl.

"No!" shouted Henry. "I'll take her - go!"

Lola froze. She couldn't bear the betrayal of another animal in this horrible drama. She shook her head.

"GO!" Henry pushed Lola up towards the ledge where Eva stood waiting. He then picked up Sona, partly draping her over his shoulder. He had only one arm wrapped around the dog, as he needed the other to steady himself, but Sona understood. She wrapped her legs around Henry as best she could and grabbed his collar with her teeth.

Lola was satisfied and scrambled out of the boat in front of him. Eva reached out, now also drenched and shivering, and pulled Lola onto the ledge with her. Eva half hugged Lola and then turned and grabbed Henry's extended hand. All three were now safe. They looked back and watched the boat at first slowly and then quickly swirl away and crash into the other side of the cove before it was sucked under and disappeared. Lola looked on in amazement.

"It is extremely deep there," Henry said quietly. "Many a small ship has met that fate. She will be in good company."

"We have to climb up to the next ledge." Eva's voice was kind, although she had to shout over the storm.

Lola appreciated Eva's calmness and familiar voice. It helped her to re-focus after the adrenaline rush of escaping from the boat.

Lola looked at the cliff. It was a steep climb, but one she could do. But Sona - Lola turned back. Henry had removed his coat and was picking up Sona again. "Tie the sleeves at my back," he requested.

Eva quickly helped him pull the coat around Sona and tied the sleeves as securely as she could.

"Lola, you go first." Eva pointed up. "Nothing you haven't already encountered in your wandering around the woods." Eva then looked at Henry. Henry motioned for her to go before him.

"No, let me take your back," Eva said still trying to sound calm over the storm. "Lola would never forgive us if the dog fell."

Henry shrugged and then began to climb after Lola. Both scrambled and pulled up - Sona hanging on and trying to stay as still as possible. At one point Lola dislodged some rubble. She turned to say sorry and nearly lost her grip.

"Keep going - don't look back," called Henry.

Lola continued. She finally reached a ledge, which was bigger and smoother than the one below, as if it had been carved out for a resting place. She had climbed twice her own height. She pulled her tired body up over the ledge scraping her stomach on the jagged edge.

Henry's head appeared moments later with Sona tied to him. Lola reached for him.

"Take Sona, I'll hurt her if I try to pull myself over," he called above the wind.

Lola carefully reached inside Henry's coat and held Sona under the front legs pulling the dog with all of her strength under the already loose coat. Lola realised that it had only just held. Sona stayed limp and quiet until Lola had her on the ledge and then she quickly recovered by shaking herself off and barking at Henry until he pulled himself clear.

They waited, but Eva did not appear. They then heard the call of a seagull overhead. Lola looked up. The cliff was leaning outward towards the sea and was as smooth as glass. Trying to climb it would be impossible.

"Isn't this where we should have someone sending ropes down?" Henry's voice carried irony, but upon his words the end of a rope thudded onto the ground in front of them. Henry looked at Lola with an apologetic smile.

Seth's owl now flew overhead. *"Tie Lola and the dog together. Use the coat to wrap them up,"* the owl sent as though he was speaking directly to Henry. Lola translated the instruction.

Henry looked reluctant at this request. He also

knew now Lola would insist and that the weight ratio would be better.

"*It's alright,*" Lola sent to Sona. "*We won't leave him behind and I won't let you go. Then I will help find Morgan for you. I will keep you safe.*"

Sona let Lola lift her and hugged close to Lola's small body while Henry tied them together with his coat. He then tied and strapped the rope around them, checking the security of each knot.

"Keep your head in towards Sona. You will swing but the more compact you are the less the injury."

Henry tugged the rope hard and Lola felt herself slowly starting to inch up and her feet beginning to dangle.

Marcus, Seth and Eva guided the rope up as they felt the weight of Lola and Sona. The King rode Shadow, who was tied to the rope, away from the cliff. Lance and The Magician looked on.

Lola felt herself in mid-air, as if she was a spider swinging from her web but not knowing where she would next catch a hold. She felt slightly queasy. The swinging was different than the rocking of the boat. The swinging started to become more intense. Sona whined slightly. "*I won't let go,*" Lola sent.

They were swinging quite dramatically now. The cliff side was coming closer and closer as they gained momentum. The rope was getting shorter and shorter as they were inched up. Lola hoped it would soon be too short to let them crash into the cliff side - then *smack!* Lola's head banged into something. She was limp and dizzy, Sona was slipping. Lola's head was spinning and her arms shaking. She tried to hold onto Sona but her arms were tangled in the coat. She could not tell which way was up. Sona had slipped down to her waist and her back feet were now pressing on Lola's boots while her front paws started scraping Lola's shoulders. Sona was whining and crying. Lola could now taste blood and felt something warm trickling down the side of her face. Then something or someone separated them and pulled Lola over the top of the ledge.

Suddenly Sona was whining and rushing around Lola's body trying to lick a cut that was on the side of Lola's head, where it had smashed into the cliff.

Lola looked up. She could feel someone supporting her shoulder. Her vision was blurred. There, in front of her, was the fuzzy outline of an old man's head. His hair was pushed back, though a bit unkempt, and now what Lola could see were the kindest and greenest eyes she could ever have imagined.

"My dear, my dear," he half whispered, and then he hugged her.

No one had ever hugged her so deeply and so firmly. Lola felt another trickle of warm liquid down the other side of her head. She realised it was The Magician's tears.

There was someone else undoing the ropes. Soon she was free and Sona stood on one side while The Magician helped her to her feet and moved her away from the ledge. He continued to support her as she moved back. She was disorientated and confused, but she knew she was safe.

Sona stayed by the ledge as she watched Marcus lower the rope again. Sona was quiet now, but her tail quivered and you could see the anticipation in her eyes as she waited for Henry to appear over the edge.

Lola leaned against The Magician as he wrapped his cloak around her. She started to feel her legs wobble, but he was supporting her with a firm arm around her shoulders. Lola then felt a familiar cold, wet nose and silky ears slide under her hand.

"Lance," she sent, *"I made it."*

"You are an extraordinary girl." Lance now leaned into her to keep her upright.

This gave Lola more focus, just as when Isis had been on her lap or when Oskar had put his paws through the bars of her cell. It kept her from disappearing into another space, like the one she had been in when she was drugged.

Yelps now came from Sona and she was pawing the ledge. Then Henry appeared and pulled himself up and over with Marcus's and Seth's help. He had fared better than Lola, knowing how to steady and push himself over the cliff edge.

Seth was coiling the rope with Marcus. The King had now dismounted and was making his way over to Lola. He beckoned to The Magician.

"Come, get up onto Shadow with her. Let's get out of this storm," the King called out.

Eva was now with them too. She tore a piece of her scarf and wrapped it around Lola's head. Lola was then lifted, with the help of Marcus and Henry onto Shadow's back to sit in front of The Magician.

"Try to stay awake, my dear." The Magician's voice was slow and steady again. "It's not far and you should have a herbal mixture before you sleep to heal the wound. Just a little longer and then you can sleep like you haven't for some time. We will wait until you are well enough to travel before we leave The Forest Castle."

Lola realised that The Magician's talk was just him trying to keep her from passing out.

"Head injuries," he continued, "you need to stay conscious until we can get the blood flow right. And there will be soup, I'm sure you missed my soup. You can't go to sleep without having had some of my soup."

The Magician was trying to gently rock Lola as they went along. He looked down at Eva, who was walking along beside them, and quietly said, "Better go and warn Steed."

Eva knowingly nodded and then discretely melted into the woods.

Steed knew that they must be coming soon. The Forest Castle had expanded slightly to make room for more guests. Three wolves came running up the path. The two who were his companions had come for a fuss, and then Eva was standing in front of him.

"They are not far, maybe twenty minutes," she said. "Lola is hurt, we will need some special herbs boiled. Can we stoke the fire?"

"Of course, my lady." Steed disappeared inside the

large oak arch, Eva following.

As Steed went in, two small animals came out. Aya escorted Pixey to the hinged side of the doorway.

"Sit in front of me, but straight up. She will see that you have grown." Aya gave Pixey's head a quick lick. It was a habit that Aya acquired from being part of a litter of kittens. It almost felt like Sophie to Pixey, only a bit softer.

The wolves stationed themselves a bit further down the track, at the bend where you turned to see the Forest Castle in front of you. The snow was falling heavily now and sticking to their coats, making them look like they were fringed with white fur.

"There, you have some friends waiting to welcome you," The Magician said quietly as Shadow turned around the bend.

"Welcome back, Lola," Ebony sent. *"We are pleased you are safe."*

"But you are troubled." Dawn took a step deeper into Lola's mind. *"You have lost a friend in your escape to safety."*

Dawn's ability to penetrate Lola's mind shook her into a more conscious state. Her head really hurt now. *"Yes, he was the truest of friends,"* Lola sent back and she knew that Dawn could picture Oskar in her mind.

"I'm sad for you," Ebony now sent having picked up Dawn's observation. *"I know what loss is."*

The two wolves walked either side of Shadow to the gateway of the Forest Castle where there was a natural opening in a hedge of holly. Marcus helped Lola down and he and The Magician supported her. Both wolves passed under her hands in an affectionate, but respectful way and then disappeared into the woods towards the eastern hills.

Lola looked up at the castle. It was an oak tree, but the most enormous of oak trees. It was a completely different shape than it had been the last time she was there. It had windows around the sides and there was the smell of a fire and food cooking. Yes, the smell of soup and bread wafted out of the window to the right of the large door in front of them.

"How can this be?" Lola almost gasped.

"It is what the Forest Castle does. It accommodates anyone who visits," The Magician smiled.

Then Lola looked down at the two small animals sitting in front of the door. *"Pixey!"* Lola sent. *"You should have said you would be here."*

"I've grown and I wanted it to be a surprise," Pixey answered.

"She is quite brave now," Aya sent.

Lola dropped to her knees and reached out to Pixey, who stood up and stretched and then gently walked over to Lola and began to purr and rub up against Lola's hands and arms and legs. Even with all of her disorientation and physical pain, the sound of Pixey purring, her smell, her soft fur, all of it made Lola feel as if the world was completely right again. Pixey jumped into Lola's arms. The Magician helped Lola up again.

"Come, my dear. Herbal tea, soup and then the

softest of beds for you."

They went into the Forest Castle. The others followed.

The Forest Castle was able to accommodate anyone or anything. Had it been a royal entourage from some great nation, it would have supplied a great marble-floored hall with chandeliers and a banqueting table. But this was a group of relatively humble friends who happened to have the responsibility of keeping their farms and villages safe within the valleys that they lived in. This they did very well. They were a reflection of all that was good and wholesome in the world. Even the King desired simplicity over grandeur.

So, they entered a homely farmhouse kitchen with the table laid. There were fresh bread roles in a basket, fresh creamy butter and soup simmering on a range built into a large fireplace. It was warm, even the floor was warm in contrast with the snowy scene outside.

Lola immediately felt relieved. There were people she knew, smells she knew and Pixey in her arms. How, she wondered to herself, did she get through those last days? It seemed as if she had been away for a year. Yet it was barely few weeks since she had been in this very place, subduing the serpents. She could feel them, but they seemed to pose no threat.

Eva immediately came over to Lola and led her to the chair nearest the fire. Lola sat in it, still wrapped in The Magician's cloak, with Pixey now on her lap. Eva gave her a small brown mug filled with a clear liquid. It smelled of lavender and sage, but she wasn't sure what else. Its taste was bitter, but somehow pleasant. There was honey in it too, trying to soften that bitterness. Eva had a clean white cloth that she had soaked in witch hazel. She gently pressed it against Lola's head. It smarted, but Lola could feel it pulling out the possibility of infection, so she remained still.

"You are much thinner, my dear," said The Magician as he put half a bowl of soup in front of Lola. "Only eat a small amount at first. There will always be more later." He turned to Henry. "I would advise the same for you, Henry. Too much can do more harm than too little after what you have both been through."

Henry nodded, still feeling both dazed but relieved that they survived.

Lola followed The Magician's gaze. Henry did look thin and drawn. She pictured him as an active healthy man who spent a lot of time outdoors, but his dark skin was ashen and grey circles shadowed his eyes.

"You are right, old friend," said Henry, pausing, but actually wanting to eat the whole pot of soup. "I shall see how much this fills me for now." He pushed away the small bowl that he had had and sipped warm water from the tankard Steed had given him.

Sona too was given a small amount of ground meat and porridge with the intention of her just having a few spoonfuls regularly throughout the evening.

Marcus and Seth sat at the end of the table, feeling slightly guilty as they devoured large bowls of soup and a loaf of bread between them. Lola glanced at them with a knowing smile. It was the first time she had ever seen them eat anything that wasn't cooked by Milly.

The Magician's advice was sound. Lola felt full after just a small amount of soup and half a piece of bread, but the taste of both was exquisite. She savoured each mouthful as if she had been given heavenly nectar. Upon finishing, she was given a spoonful of The Magician's most potent honey, which cured everything from infection to low spirits.

"Bed now," Eva smiled as she reached out her hand to help Lola stand. They left the men to discuss what dangers might be threatening the Three Valleys and to inform Henry on Morgan's welfare.

Lola still had Pixey on her lap and she scooped the kitten up as she took Eva's hand. Lola felt steadier and clearer after the tea and the food, but she could also feel the serpents whispering more intensely.

She hadn't left them behind on the other side of the mountains.

Eva noticed that Lola looked slightly disturbed. "There is no way to completely stop them whispering to you. Keep Pixey with you as an anchor. I will sit with you while you sleep and The Magician will sit with them to try to calm them. They did tell us you were coming. They are not all bad."

Eva and Lola walked slowly down the corridor. The walls looked as if they had been made out of the inside of an oak tree. The floor was made of soft, warm moss. Every once in a while they passed a small round window that revealed the snow falling thickly in the dimming light. They passed a number of doors made of oak with black iron hinges shaped like oak leaves, similar to those in the King's castle. As they came to the end of this corridor the whispering lessened.

When they arrived at the very last room, Eva opened the door. It was of a generous size and held an oak bed piled with soft white pillows and quilts. Behind a curtain, a slight waft of steam escaped and the smell of lavender and chamomile permeated the room.

"Here, let's put Pixey on the bed for her own ablutions. I will help you bath." Eva was still supporting Lola.

For once in her life, Lola relished having a bath. Eva carefully brushed and then washed her hair. The smell of lavender and chamomile calmed Lola and, when Eva finally helped her into a clean white shift, Lola curled up in the luxury of the bed with Pixey purring by her side. Eva towel dried and brushed through her hair until it was only damp.

As Lola fell into a deep dreamless sleep, she could just hear the howling of wolves high up in the mountains. They were telling of her escape and how a loyal dog had helped her. The dog, they howled, must be found and kept safe. When possible, the dog must be brought to her.

The whispering of the serpents now barely touched her mind.

CHAPTER 19

Magic and Snow

It snowed heavily over the next few days. Lola rested during this time, carefully attended by Eva and The Magician. Henry and Sona also rested, though they met regularly with the King, Seth and Marcus.

Sona and Lance found themselves with much to share, somewhat to the distraction of the King, who now saw one of the drawbacks of being in two places at once. He found himself having started a conversation about military strategies whilst, at the same time, a discussion about chasing rabbits or rodents was going on between Sona and Lance.

Lola giggled when he went to her for advice and said she understood, but the only thing you could do was get used to it. She added that maybe Lance was experiencing the same frustration. "Rodents may be far more important to him than military strategies," she advised, "after all, he is a dog."

One thing that was clear from these meetings was that, once spring came, the Middle Valley would be under threat of attack. The snows now made it impossible by land and extremely unlikely by sea. Patrols, though, would be kept on the beaches, both in the Middle Valley and the Western Valley. Though difficult, travel between the valleys was feasible, especially if the snow was packed down by the first set of troops.

"We haven't been attacked for more than a hundred years," the King commented while sitting at the large oak table in the kitchen.

"The treasures will have to be protected," The Magician added. "We are here for them more than any other reason."

"Who will do that?" asked Marcus.

The Magician was quiet for a moment and then looked down the corridor towards Lola's room. "I have never had to hide them, but I was given instructions by my grandfather. There must be three of us and the youngest must open the gate. No trace of treasure can be left this side of it and, when it is safe to do so, it must be put back in our keeping as quickly as possible." He looked down the corridor again. "I hope she will be strong enough. We will need to do it at sun-return. Let's hope the snows keep us safe until then."

"That is barely a few weeks away," said Seth.

"And you have to get to the other side of the kingdom by then," added Marcus.

Steed was quietly working a piece of wood in the corner of the kitchen by the fire. He looked up. "I once heard about magic carpets from my queen. She used to tell me stories when I was still very young. She was like a mother to my brother and I when we first came here. We wanted to see one, but she didn't know anyone who would visit and show us one. Then one day she had a visitor in the winter. We thought he was on a magic carpet because he glided over the snow. Kyle and I studied what he rode and together we made one. I know now they are called sleighs, but we thought it was our version of a magic carpet."

The others looked at him and smiled. "Of course," said the King. "I always remember the Forest Queen gliding in and gliding away when she visited in the winter."

"I can see you home in it if you like," Steed said to The Magician.

"And this valley? Who will anchor the serpents?" the King asked.

Eva had walked into the room now. "I can stay with the wolves until Steed's return," she suggested. "My journey back will be much quicker."

The Magician was quiet for a moment. "I would rather not risk it; we need to be together at sun-return."

"I can stay," said Henry. "I know this castle and I know these woods well. I even know these serpents."

"He does," said Steed. "We have had Henry visit many times."

The King looked surprised. "But your daughter," he said.

"I would like my daughter to find me here. We would both be more comfortable here than in the King's castle."

Lance furrowed his brow and whined slightly with concern. He had become used to Sona's company and was looking forward to them all being at the King's castle. Henry sensed this.

"Take Sona with you and send them back together. My daughter is an excellent horse-woman."

"What about the Serpent Lord's daughter?" asked the King.

"It is up to her. I am happy to look after her here, but she may want to stay with you in the Middle Valley."

The King pondered for a moment. "I suppose it would mean they were both safe for the time being. An attack would come from one of the beaches. This way Lola, Eva and The Magician would be safe in their caves also."

"Lola must be kept from any fighting," said The Magician. "But you are likely to need me."

"If you are lost, how do we retrieve the treasure?" asked the King.

"A third must be found," replied The Magician. "Perhaps the new Forest Queen, when one emerges, along with Eva and Lola."

"And what if the Forest Queen is one in the same of these three?" questioned Eva. She did not name Lola or herself, but she knew that they were likely heirs to become the new Forest Queen. This could make being part of the three people who had hidden the treasure complicated. Rituals on the longest day would determine this, but Eva worried that Lola was not ready. She had been through too much and still had months of training to do with Eva in order to become skilled enough to develop her mind and control the forces in both the inner and outer worlds.

"Somehow the right person will emerge in my absence. No one is indispensable. Life always carries on. Every loss is an opportunity for something new to arise," replied The Magician.

"Well, there is no battle yet," said the King. "This is all just speculation. We just do the next thing we need to do and that is to be sure everyone is where they should be at sun-return. I will ride back with your daughter and her companion, Henry. I am sure one of my knights will gladly join us while the other escorts Lola, Eva and The Magician home." The King looked at Marcus and Seth with a mischievous air.

The next day Lola woke and got ready for the journey. Eva made sure she was wrapped and dressed warmly in the clothes that Milly had made. She had a dark red wool dress with a lighter red cloak. It was edged with the darker hue of her dress. Lola also wore her beloved boots, which seemed to have miraculously been cleaned of the salt from the sea and the filth of the prison.

Steed had the sleigh ready. Two majestic black and white horses, even bigger than the plough horses on Lola's father's farm, stood ready to pull the beautifully carved wooden sleigh. The wood was honey coloured and polished throughout with bee's wax. As with much of the ornamentation around the Forest Castle, intricate carvings of oak leaves and acorns decorated the sides. There were two generous-sized seats in it covered with light olive green velvet.

Marcus helped Lola up into the back seat. Though

her head was much better, the ordeal of her journey, being drugged and nearly starved, was evident.

Steed now looked at Eva and The Magician. "Who would like to sit up here and help me drive?" he asked politely, assuming it would be Eva, as The Magician, being older, would want to relax in the back and keep warm.

"Oh, I shall do that," The Magician immediately chimed. "I haven't been in a sleigh for many years." His twinkling eyes gave away his delight at the prospect.

Eva laughed. "I thought so," she said as she climbed into the back with Lola and handed over Pixey. The three of them nestled down under a thick wool blanket that matched their cushioned seats.

Marcus rode Coal, the King rode Shadow and Seth rode his own horse, Red, who was actually a rusty brown colour, although she did shine red in the sunlight. Henry would look after the other horse Eva had ridden.

Sona, Lance and Aya were to go on foot, unless the snow became too deep. Then they would join Lola and Eva in the sleigh.

Henry waved them off. Dawn and Ebony made a brief appearance. The serpents were quiet today. The Magician had tried his best to guard Lola from hearing their whispers while they were at the Forest Castle. Lola turned and looked towards the eastern mountains. They were still and covered with snow. She had tried to send to Oskar, but he was very far away, and few animals could send that far. Pixey and

Sophie were the only ones who could do it successfully with her. Yet the call of wolves kept telling the story of how he should be found and brought to her. Was he up there somewhere, trying to find her? No, nothing stirred in her eyes' view.

Steed whipped the reigns and the horses started. The snow all around was deep, but the huge animals almost seemed to scamper over it, hardly sinking in at all and packing down the snow at the same time for the other horses to follow, not to mention the fox and the dogs.

"How are they doing that?" asked Lola, amazed at the spectacle of their huge feathered-like hoofs dancing in the snow.

"A little magic left behind by the Forest Queen I think," Eva smiled. "This sleigh really is like a magic carpet."

"Go well, Lola, you will be safe for now," Lola heard a light, kind voice say. She looked around to see who it was. She caught a quick glimpse of a small woman in a green gown and a waterfall of auburn hair disappearing into the woods.

Eva followed Lola's gaze. "She will stay here in some form while the new Forest Queen comes into her own power. Then she will pass to the next realm," Eva said.

"What is the next realm?" asked Lola. "Is it like where I saw my mother?"

"Maybe," replied Eva. "Those who have passed often appear to us in a space that we can understand.

What they see and experience, though, may be very different."

The sleigh was now speeding through the woods. Lola felt a chill on her cheeks. More than once she leaned over to warm her face on Pixey's soft fur. Pixey was in the warmest place, shielded by the blanket on Lola's lap. She knew this and had every intention of keeping it that way. She complained slightly when Lola tried to position her so that she could take in the scenery.

The Magician was in his element. Steed was hardly needed. He handled the reigns as if he had done this all his life, whistling and clicking at the magnificent horses and chuckling and cheering at every bend.

Eva was relieved to see The Magician so happy. Having Lola back and being on the way home had greatly cheered him. Having deep snow to stop him worrying about intruders to The Valleys until spring and a ride in a magic sleigh cheered him even more. Eva sat back slightly, leaning into Lola for warmth and watched the snow-encrusted trees sail by. The woods were beautiful and she was with those she loved. Sometimes this was a conflict for her, going against her love of solitude, but just now she too was immensely cheered by the sleigh ride.

The horses made the ride go very quickly. They even seemed to pull the others along with them. Steed explained to the King that once they had made a path it would be sound and passable until the next snow. This boded well for the King's return journey with

Morgan.

Sona did tire. She too was still recovering from her ordeal in the Serpent Lord's dungeons. She nestled herself at Eva and Lola's feet. Pixey kept an eye on her occasionally. She was so different to Lance or Aya but, after a while, Pixey decided that she did quite like her and returned her attention once again to nestling in the blanket.

Hardly half the day had gone by when they reached the bridge that marked the boundary between the Eastern and Middle Valleys. Lola wondered how they would get over it as it was essentially a footbridge, though it could take a horse and one rider.

The river was partially frozen, but the sound of running water could still be easily heard. Steed took the reigns whilst The Magician called out a short incantation. Rather than going over the bridge, the sleigh aimed straight for the river. As the sleigh reached the bank, the snow and ice thickened, making a secure path for the sleigh, which glided across just like a magic carpet.

That part of the sleigh's enchantment only lasted a few moments. Aya, Lance and the rest of the party had to make use of the bridge. Steed waited until everyone was successfully across until he started up again.

After a few more miles, the King hailed them. Perhaps it was time for a rest, he suggested.

"Not too long," said Steed. "We don't want the horses to cool off too much." He then went to a drawer underneath the sleigh and took out a blanket for each horse in turn to keep them warm during the rest. "When we get to the castle, they will need twenty-four hours to rest before they can carry on."

Bread, cheese and some dried fruit refreshed everyone, but it was only a brief stop and soon they were on their way again. Lola remembered the escape through these woods, which seemed so long ago. She was a different person now. She had travelled further than most people in these valleys, though not willingly. Now every tree and stone they passed was one more step closer to her home. She had actually enjoyed her stay at the Forest Castle, even with the constant whispering of the serpents. But the closer they came to the King's castle and surrounding fields, the more she was sure she just wanted to be home with the occasional visit to the castle to see her friends. Pixey agreed as she read Lola's thoughts and began to purr loudly.

Soon the King's castle was in sight from the tops of the far fields. Aya sent Lola a discrete thought, that she would find them all later, and disappeared into the hedges. The horses and sleigh carried on to the castle gates. Everyone dismounted and got down from the sleigh. Steed, Marcus and Seth led the horses.

"We'll see you later," Marcus smiled at Lola as she followed The Magician and Eva into the courtyard, behind the King and Lance. Pixey was still wrapped in Lola's cloak, enjoying being close to Lola, and had no intention of losing her person again. Lance and Sona walked side by side in front of the King.

Suddenly Sona began to whine, bark, jump and almost dance. Then she raced up the steps of the castle to where the great doors were opening. There stood Morgan and Ariella. Sona raced to Morgan who fell to her knees on the frozen steps to embrace her. Sona could hardly contain herself. She briefly rushed over to Ariella, jumping up and licking her cheek, much to Ariella's surprise, before returning and rushing circles around Morgan, licking her hands and face and being sure that she was scenting her thoroughly so she would not lose her again.

"Her connection with Morgan is as strong as mine is with the King," Lance sent to Lola. *"Their separation must have been very painful."*

"Yes," returned Lola, *"and mine from Pixey, yet I shut it out to have enough strength to escape."* She held Pixey closer. *"I'm sorry Pixey. We shall both get stronger so we don't have to ever let go of each other again."*

Lola then thought of The Magician's words: 'The two strongest human emotions are love and fear. Of the two love is stronger, we just don't give it a chance.' Lola had been afraid to feel for those she loved in the Serpent Lord's dungeons. She hugged Pixey again. *"Next time, I'll be brave enough to keep loving,"* she sent. Only she really hoped that there would be no next time.

Milly now appeared on the steps with Sophie lingering behind. Sophie wasn't sure about the frantic collie making a fuss of Morgan. Milly, however, didn't even notice Sona and Morgan, but went straight to Lola and hugged her as tight as she could without crushing Pixey. She then held her away to look at her. "Oh my dear, I knew those colours would suit you, and bless the day as you are here to wear them. Oh, my dear." Milly hugged Lola again.

Eva, the King and The Magician were now at the top of the stairs with Lance joining in, prancing around everyone. "Let us go inside and find a warm fire," said the King.

Milly held onto Lola, leading her along with the rest. The King walked with Morgan and the dogs, half amused by Lance still insisting on escorting Sona.

Morgan noticed Lance's attention and knelt down. "You see, I told you. She is one of the best dogs ever." Morgan stroked Lance's forehead and ears, which he loved.

He sat for just a moment, regarding Morgan's deep brown eyes, and then was up again, escorting Sona, but trying to give everyone else his attention as well.

Ariella discretely scooped up Sophie as they walked along. She found herself walking beside The Magician. "She is the sweetest of cats," Ariella said to The Magician as she held back a bit from the rest of the group to keep Sophie away from the dogs.

"Yes, yes she is, and a very brave little cat too." The Magician lingered also and stroked Sophie's chin.

Ariella still held back. She looked at The Magician directly. "All of these things that happened with the serpents here, could they have happened as a story in my father's kingdom? Why are there wells in both places?" she asked.

"Well, that is a very complex matter," The Magician explained. "The serpents are creatures of the underworld, the part of us that exists under our everyday awareness. In these valleys, which are a reflection of what is best in the world, they have always been controlled and channeled by the Forest Queen. She pacifies them so that they have enough attention, but not too much control. What happened to the Forest Queen seems to me almost impossible without some other influence, very strong influence, coming from somewhere else in the world. Yet, the end of the reign of a Forest Queen is never the same, particularly as there never is anyone alive who knows exactly what may happen in the process."

"M-mm." Ariella was deep in thought for a moment, then she gently put down Sophie and looked back up at The Magician. "You know, I used to talk to them all the time. I was little. I used to play in my father's hall and watch the well and they would talk to me. They told me stories of fantastic places and creatures. Then I became older and father said I had to be more of a lady and couldn't run around the hall playing. I thought father was looking old and unhappy more and more of the time, but my uncle told me not to say anything in front of him. Then the boy Umir came. The one who told stories and who would sometimes write day and night. When he finished, he would then read to father. I was often listening from behind the black velvet curtains. I realise now he was telling the story of

Lola subduing the serpents."

"Yes, Lola has spoken a little of this boy to me," said The Magician. "She said he was quite young but could write better than anyone she knew. Of course Lola doesn't know many people who can read and write so it is hard to tell what this boy can do, but it sounds like he is deeply connected with her in some way."

"Perhaps." Ariella kept walking in the sight of the others. "I must admit I didn't give him much thought, other than listening to his story. Father suddenly was giving him all the attention, as if Umir was able to tell him how to control the serpents, yet I had been communicating with them since I could remember. I listened to Umir's story because hearing adventure stories always made me feel happy." Ariella stopped. She looked down at the rough stone on the floor that they walked upon. It was not like the polished floors in her father's palace. There was character and friendliness about these stones. She smiled and then looked up again. "I never thought I would be in an adventure story, which I suppose now I am."

"I'm afraid the adventure might become more rigorous as spring arrives. Your uncle is likely to attack our valleys and try to capture Lola on your father's behalf again. We, of course, now know how to keep her safe, but what of you? Morgan will join her father at the Forest Castle. Will you go with them? I would feel much happier if you were away from any fighting."

"Will father come for me?" Ariella felt embarrassed. She didn't want to go back really. There seemed little for her in her father's world. She looked at the stone floor again. She liked being somewhere where the stone looked friendly and had character. She treasured the thought of being amongst friends, but was not sure this would remain the case if her uncle attacked.

"I'm afraid your father has been taken ill," explained The Magician, as kindly as he could. "He tried to touch the serpents. He thought he would be able to get close to them."

Ariella froze for a moment; then she asked, "Will he live?"

"I don't know. I didn't see it happen, but Lola did." The Magician looked down the hall. The others had now sat in front of one of the large fires. The dogs had finally settled down on one of the rugs. "We will rest here tomorrow. Lola will need to be quiet tonight, but I'm sure you could ask her more about what happened tomorrow."

"Yes, yes I will," said Ariella, looking towards the gathering at the fire. She felt she wanted to drop all thoughts of home and just be in the castle with the others, even the dogs. "Shall we join them?" she suggested to The Magician. "I hear there will be Milly's honey cakes."

"Yes, perhaps we should." The Magician led the way.

Morgan was sitting next to the King when Ariella and The Magician joined the gathering. The King was quietly telling Morgan of her father's welfare and that her father wanted her to join him at the Forest Castle.

The King went on to explain that Lola would go with The Magician and Eva to the Western Valley for sun-return, and that, once he himself had escorted her to the Forest Castle, he would return to the Middle Valley. It was hoped that, with her and her father along with Steed and the wolves there would be balance across The Three Valleys for sun-return, as Henry was a long-standing friend of the Forest Queen before she was taken by the serpents.

They were quiet now, with everyone staring into the fire and nibbling on honey biscuits, dried fruit, or cheese and relishes. The magical adventure through the sparkling woodlands had left everyone in a reflective mood.

Ariella sat beside Lola. She smiled and took Lola's hand for a moment, but said nothing.

Eva broke the silence. "Lola, we shall stay in the castle tonight. You still need someone to watch out for you while you sleep."

"But …"

"We are all staying in the castle by night my dear," said Milly. "I'll be just down the hall, as usual." Milly had made up a bed for herself in her laundry room. She still checked her cottage in the day and cooked there and tended her garden, but it was decided that everyone connected with the taming of the serpents had to be under guard at night and never alone. This included Ariella and Morgan. Although they were by no means seen as part of the enemy, they posed a threat in that someone might try to come for them.

Soon the gathering broke for bed. The Magician stopped Ariella again. "Once the snows really begin it will be almost impossible to come back to this castle until spring. You will be safe at the Forest Castle, but isolated," he explained.

"I shall think about it," she said and gave a slight bow of her head as a goodnight gesture.

CHAPTER 20

A Meeting

Lola sat with Pixey on the window seat in the western corridor of the castle. The hills that she had come through with The Magician only a few months ago were now covered with snow. The last leaves hanging had been encased in a wintry blanket. She loved the castle and her friends in it, but she was glad they were only spending a day to rest. She so wanted to return to the cottage in the Western Valley, and be able to amble through the woods and visit Eva in her caves. She knew she would be able to make her way up to the caves, no matter the weather, because she had always watched the foxes who she now knew were Eva, the cats, and oh yes, one fox. She was interested in Eva's ability to change, but she had no desire to change herself.

Lola's right hand gently glided down from her lap to stroke Lance every once in a while. Pixey lay curled up with Lola's left hand wrapped around the kitten to keep her from slipping towards the window.

"Time to make our way home," Lola sent to Pixey. *"We have been through quite enough for one autumn. Now it is winter and you shall see. We shall curl up each night in front of the fire and the cottage will smell of baking bread,*

mulled cider and of course, The Magician's soup. I suppose he will be teaching me to read and write again. I think I can bear that after all I've been through."

Pixey simply purred, acknowledging Lola's thoughts, just happy to have her back and not having to think about too much of anything, except what they were doing at that moment.

Lola heard a door open and shut at the end of the corridor. As the low winter sunlight entered each window it reflected on Ariella's fair face and dark hair as she walked towards Lola. How could someone so lovely be the daughter of such an intimidating man, thought Lola. She shuddered at the memory of him glaring at her every time she looked up when Umir was reading his story.

"Hello Lola," Ariella said quietly. "I was hoping to find you alone."

Lola gave a shy smile. She hardly felt alone in her mind, but a dog and a cat were not cause for concern in Ariella's mind in relation to privacy.

Ariella continued. "I wanted to talk to you about my father." Ariella looked down and took a deep breath, before looking back at Lola. "First of all, I wanted to say how deeply, deeply sorry I am for all that you have been through. I know my father's dungeons are a wretched place and you did well to escape. Not many do." Ariella's voice had trailed off and she was again looking downwards.

Lola sat up and adjusted Pixey. "Come, sit here," Lola said, patting a space on the cushion beside herself.

"I expect you would like news of your father."

"Yes, I would." Ariella looked up again. She smiled shyly and then sat down to share the window seat with Lola.

"I cannot pretend I admired you father, Ariella, but I did pity him. He wanted power from the serpents and was consumed by their presence. It meant he could care for little else. I can see that now. Umir, who he seemed to be fostering, was not really important. He was interested only in what Umir could do to help him control the serpents."

"I know that, Lola," returned Ariella. "I disappeared in my father's eyes many years ago. I simply became a thing to trade, like a well-bred horse or dog. But what did the serpents do to him? I had heard Umir's story. I knew you, or of you. A girl who had tamed and then banned the serpents from causing evil in these valleys. That meant that they appeared in our well in a more solid form. That made father ecstatic. He thought he was truly the heir to the power they had, but he couldn't control them. I'm sure that is why he came to find you."

"I think now I understand what happened," Lola said. "When I told the serpents they could not appear or influence the world, the world in my mind was only these three valleys. That was all that I pictured in my thoughts. I had no idea about other places so my imagination could not bind them in other lands."

"I see, so they just needed to find somewhere that you could not imagine and then they could reemerge there."

"Yes, I think so. Of course, your father's hall is one of the closest places to the Forest Castle that they could emerge and it was completely outside of my imagination."

"How was father taken ill?" asked Ariella.

"He tried to touch them. You cannot touch them. You cannot go near them safely unless you have the support of another with whom you have a strong connection. With that other you must bind a ring of light around their well. Then you can communicate with them."

Ariella was quiet for a moment. "I used to talk to them. I would walk around the well and hear their voices. They told stories of many places, places of magic and adventure. They were my only source of creativity and imagination. I used to play in the hall. Oh, the floor was so cold – but, nonetheless, it was a huge space to run around in and you could slide across that marble with your stocking feet."

Lola looked at Ariella in amazement. She had hated the black marble floor, but even she had to admit that, in stocking feet, it would take on a whole other use that Lola hadn't thought of. "I'm not sure I can imagine playing in that hall. It must have been very strange," said Lola.

"It wasn't strange if it was all you knew," replied Ariella.

"How did the serpents talk to you? Did you hear their voices in your mind or did they speak out loud?" asked Lola.

"Oh, it was definitely in my mind. Father never knew I was listening to them," said Ariella. "He never heard them say anything to him, just saw their ethereal forms and lots of billowing vapour coming out of the well. It wasn't until he saw them become solid that he became so excited about being able to control them."

"How did having the well in the hall come about?" asked Lola.

"It was always there. I don't even think my father or my grandfather, who I can only just remember, knew. They just always had the well and always had the view that it was their destiny to control the serpents over anyone else, but didn't know how. My father had many wise men come and go, giving him advice on it. When he acted on their advice he would think that he had power over them for a little while, but then he'd realise that he didn't. He even had advice once on how to find a woman who would come and show him, but it was never acted upon successfully."

"I wonder if they meant the Forest Queen, but she would never have let herself be taken in that way. She would have sensed their every intention if they had tried."

"I think perhaps someone did. I remember my uncle being furious with father about a boat that was lost, that hadn't brought 'her' back."

"They would have tried to climb the sailor's folly," said Lola pensively and then looked at Ariella. "It looks like there is a way up from the cliffs in the Eastern Valley, yet it brings you to a whirlpool and only leads half way up the cliff. Anyone trying to go to the Eastern Valley that way would have lost their boats, and eventually their lives on the cliffs.

Both girls were quiet for a moment, then Lola asked, "Will you go with Morgan to the Forest Castle?"

"No, I think it would be best if I stayed here. Morgan does not need to be my keeper. She should have time with her father alone. If my uncle attacks on the pretense that he is rescuing me, I want to be sure I can present myself freely to stop any conflict."

"Do you want to go back?"

"Not really, but I don't want anyone else hurt in my name either."

"You are brave, Ariella," smiled Lola.

"I am learning," replied Ariella. "Learning to think beyond what I have always been told is right or wrong. I still have so much to learn."

The girls fell silent again and both reflected on the conversation. They watched the sun slip beyond the mountains in the Western Valley.

Later a simple supper was given to everyone and then they took an early night before a day of travel that would see the valleys balanced again ready for sun-return.

Morgan went to sleep as soon as she could, with Sona at her side, deep in the anticipation that the next day she would see her father again.

Ariella did not have a day's travel ahead. She sat by the fire a little longer, dressed for bed, but not yet ready to succumb to sleep. In her dressing gown pocket she pulled out the cone that The Magician had said belonged to the sequoia tree. She smiled and marveled at it. How could one of those gigantic trees be hiding inside the cone? But he assured her one did. The Magician was an honest man, she thought to herself. She continued to sit and marvel at it until the cold of the night finally took her to her bed.

CHAPTER 21

Reunited

The horses and the wonderful sleigh were waiting at dawn. It had not snowed again so the King and Morgan were assured of a worn path through the woods back to the Forest Castle. Lance was excited and ready to escort Sona back. Knowing he would have to leave her with her mistress for the winter months, he was determined to enjoy their journey together to the full.

Steed had readied the sleigh with The Magician as his co-pilot again. As usual, Sophie had said goodbye to everyone early and was now nowhere to be seen. Thomas had organised Primo and Bella to be part of the farewell party at the castle gates. Milly stood with Ariella, entreating that it had been too short and loading the sleigh with more blankets and clothing for Lola. Pixey had her seat wrapped in Lola's cloak and was ready to ride in comfort.

Marcus was to accompany Lola, Eva and The Magician on Coal and then return with Steed. Seth was on Red again to accompany the King and Morgan. The King, of course, rode Shadow and Morgan was on a beautiful black and white mare called Brigit. Aya was nowhere to be seen, which troubled Marcus slightly.

Goodbyes were said quickly as daylight this time of year was limited and both parties wanted to do their journeys in the light as much as possible.

The Magician's delight was as apparent this day as it had been two days before. He took the reigns for most of the journey, which seemed to go very quickly although they were taking the track around the mountain. As before, Marcus felt pulled along by the sleigh as he followed, and Coal didn't tire. They stopped only briefly and then were again on their way.

The sun was just disappearing behind the mountains when Lola smelt wood smoke. They were now heading down the valley to The Magician's cottage.

"Who would have known we were coming?" Lola asked Eva as she realised they were finally nearing the cottage.

"I don't know," replied Eva, "it isn't me this time."

Before long, the sleigh pulled into the front garden of the cottage. A light glow came from inside. There was the smell of bread and stew seeping through the cracks in the lintels around the front door.

Eva, Lola and The Magician all looked at each other. Marcus and Steed took the horses and let the other three travelers make their way into the cottage.

The Magician was the first in the door to discover Lola's father sitting by the fire with Leo on his lap.

Lola's father stood as The Magician entered with a look of anticipation on his face. "I did as you said, sir," he explained. "I milked my cows, I tended my sheep, and I kept Lola in my mind all the time. I came here to see to the cat and the goat every few nights. Our dear Stella said she had an inkling that you might return and sent me up with the stew."

The Magician smiled and stepped forward. Lola was able to step into the cottage behind him then. Her father's look of anticipation became relief. He stretched out his arms and Lola went towards him, dropping Pixey on The Magician's chair beside Leo. Her father hugged her as deeply and securely as The Magician had when he pulled her off the cliff edge. This time it was her own tears that Lola felt trickling down her face.

Eva discretely said her goodbyes once they had eaten and made her way back up to her caves, feeling relieved at the prospect of a few days' solitude. Marcus and Steed went to sleep in the loft of the barn in readiness for a dawn start. Lola went out with them briefly to reunite with Nanny to whom she promised she would tell everything in the morning. The fresh hay that her father had obviously laid in Nanny's stable was inviting to Lola and she would have made her bed there that night had it not been for the freezing temperature and Pixey waiting for her in her own loft.

Before Lola returned to the cottage, Marcus stopped her. Out of his pocket he pulled the two ribbons he had taken from her ladder. "Here, you should put these back. They kept the bond yet again," he said, as he enclosed them in her small hands which he held affectionately for a moment.

Through the night, Lola's father dozed in The Magician's chair. In the morning he was gone without a word. Thus everything was back to the way it had been a few weeks before.

*   *   *   *   *   *   *   *

The journey east for the King and Morgan was uneventful. Henry was right. Morgan was a good rider and held her own on Brigit, alongside Red and Shadow. The path laid by the sleigh seemed to ease the way with little need to rest. Even the dogs managed to keep up, prancing along and, at times, even playing a game of chase. More than once the King had to remind Lance to focus rather than play, as Lance's antics sometimes disturbed the King from his own concentration.

Seth led with his owls flying in stages. They could cover much more distance than the horses. They were charged with reporting back on any trouble, but there was none to report. Mostly they flew for a short time and then dozed in a tree while they waited for the horses to catch up.

Morgan and the King chatted as they went. Morgan had been wary of the King in the castle and all that seemed to go with his station but, out in the woods on his horse, he just seemed an ordinary man. They talked of horses and dogs. The King asked Morgan about sailing, which interested him, though he had never mastered it. He delighted in her honest smile and laughter. She didn't put on any airs and graces to impress him. Her long dark hair shimmered in the sunlight in contrast with the glistening snow. She was a beautiful young woman and very robust. Her father's daughter, he thought. She belonged to everything he sensed that Henry valued; the trees, the earth, the sea, all seemed to speak as Morgan spoke.

As the King was reflecting on his delightful companion, Lance interrupted. *"Don't complain about me losing focus."*

The King looked back to see Lance and Sona trotting behind them, behaving responsibly at this point, as they proceeded through the woods.

The travelling took them into the evening. Stars started to appear through the bare trees, although the moon had not yet risen. Morgan and the King marveled at the sparkling array in the sky.

"You know that you can sail anywhere in the world and find your way back if you know the pattern of the stars," Morgan told the King.

"So I have heard," replied the King, "as if something greater and beyond us has given us an eternal map to orientate ourselves in our tiny world."

"Well put, your majesty," said Morgan, slightly in jest.

"Please." The King reached out his hand and touched Morgan's. "I am just a man who happens to be a King. Would you call me Makram? I have felt I am simply myself today. It has been a feeling that is precious to me beyond anything else."

Morgan let the King's hand firmly encase her own for a moment and then lifted it to adjust Brigit's reigns. "Makram, of course, it means noble," she replied.

"So I have been told," said the King. "I hope I live up to it."

Morgan smiled. The King could only just see the outline of her smile in the faded light. "I think perhaps you do," Morgan assured him, "in an ordinary sort of way."

"Screech!" Seth's owl was now much more active with the onset of night. *"Supper is ready and I'm going hunting."*

"We are not far, the owls have announced our coming," Seth called back.

Suddenly Morgan was filled with anticipation at seeing her father.

The King sensed this. "Come," he said, as he quickened the pace of Shadow. "I look forward to an evening of just being ordinary."

Henry was waiting at the door. The wolves discretely escorted the horses up to the gates. Having never seen Brigit before, they sensed she may not easily take to two wolves appearing, but after a few moments she understood that they were not a threat.

Morgan looked at them in amazement. She loved dogs and had had many in her life, but wolves seemed like magical creatures to her.

Morgan dismounted and greeted her father as one adventurer to another. That was how it was with them. They were not overly emotional about their meetings and partings, but did want to know all the details of each other's adventures.

They sat in the kitchen that night, comparing

stories of the voyage back to The Three Valleys, as the King began to doze in a chair by the fire, both dogs at his feet. Morgan and Henry talked of staying in the Valleys as Henry no longer would be safe in the Serpent Lord's realm.

"Besides," Henry said to Morgan, "I think we can at last live here, as I have wanted to for some time."

"Why not before?" asked Morgan.

"It would not have been fair to your mother," replied Henry.

"My mother?" questioned Morgan.

"Yes, your mother. She wasn't able to look after you Morgan, as I have told you. To see you and not be part of your life would have been torture for her. I have now learned that she has passed away and we can live here as she, in her heart of hearts, would have wanted us to."

"Passed away…" Morgan's voice trailed off and then she thought. She was feeling sadness at the loss of someone she'd never known, yet someone who had been one of the most important people in her life.

Morgan looked up at her father. "Why couldn't my mother look after me?"

"Because her station in life would have forbidden her to have a child," answered Henry.

"Why didn't you marry her then, take her away from those who would not let her be a mother?"

"She wouldn't have it. I asked her, but she wouldn't leave what she considered to be her place. It was not that she didn't love you, Morgan. She gave you your name...." Henry paused. "She just knew that you and I would be better off on our own."

Morgan sighed and took her father's hand. "I suppose we haven't done too badly," she said in a comforting tone.

When she made her way down the oak corridor, Morgan suddenly felt very strange. She felt herself as a baby and then as a woman holding a baby. Henry showed her to the room she was to stay in. It felt very familiar. She never remembered being here before, but perhaps her father had passed through on his way to the Serpent Lord's realm when she was very tiny. She had always imagined that he had sailed away with her, but perhaps he had taken her over the mountains. She settled down in her bed with Sona at her side.

As Morgan fell asleep, she felt the light touch of someone's gentle fingers brushing her hair to the side of her face. She opened her eyes a tiny bit; there was no one there.

The King lingered for a day. He and Morgan took the dogs into the surrounding woods on foot. The snow was deep, but in most places a hard crust had formed and they could walk unhindered, being much lighter than the horses.

Seth spent much of the day with Henry, helping him close down some of the outer sheds. There were a few animals that the Forest Queen had kept. There was a goat for milk and cheese and some hens. There was a lower ground room to store roots and herbs, all taken from the surrounding forest. It always made the food at the Forest Castle very unusual in taste, but appetising. Steed would be back, but Henry and Seth just liked occupying themselves out of the King's way.

The day ended with another meeting by the fire and an early night for the travelers.

At dawn the wolves appeared briefly to acknowledge the King leaving. Sona and Lance both had drooping heads, but Lance knew he must go with the King.

"The sun-return is in a few days' time," said the King as he reached down to warmly grasp the hands of Henry and Morgan in turn. "The equinox is only three months away. Not long really. The owls will come regularly to see how you are and will bring messages." He turned Shadow to follow Seth and Red. "Thank you for two delightfully ordinary days," he called back and then cantered away through the snow-shrouded woods with Lance following.

And so everyone was soon where they should be to keep the balance needed during the sun-return. The King was in his castle; The Magician in his cottage; and Steed and Henry, those who were closest to the Forest Queen, were in the Forest Castle in her absence.

CHAPTER 22

Treasure

L ola spent a few days just resting and curling up with Pixey. The Magician didn't make her read or ask for help with the cooking or cleaning. He just told her to sleep as much as she could. This she did. She walked around the cottage a little bit. She even made some snow people, and she caught up with Nanny.

The quieter Lola became in herself, the more she noticed the beauty around her. It was almost as if she was reconnecting with the night she sat in the cave with The Magician and Eva. That experience was now stronger than all of the pain and desperation of having been kidnapped.

It snowed a number of times. The Magician felt quite sure that it would be impossible for anyone to travel by sea at this time. Nonetheless, he kept a close eye and never left Lola alone.

The Magician also watched with pride at how centred and reflective Lola was becoming. "She is ready," he said quietly to himself as he watched her from the cottage kitchen. "She will manage sun-return."

It was morning. Lola climbed down from her loft

space. It had been a bitterly cold night. The frosty air penetrated the eaves and crevices of the roof. Pixey had slept close under the quilt and was now stretching out as she reached the hearthrug. The Magician had thankfully built up the fire in Lola's end of the cottage and it was pleasant to come down into warmer air and the smell of balsam wood burning.

Lola was surprised, once she had cleared the top of her steps, to see Eva sitting with a hot drink at the table quietly talking to The Magician. The sky was only just lightening. Eva must have travelled down from her caves in the dark, not that that would have been any trouble for her, Lola reminded herself. Perhaps she had been restless and decided to fly around the woods as her owl and then join them for breakfast.

"Ah, good morning, Lola." The Magician's voice was kind and quiet. "Have you slept well?"

Lola picked up Pixey, who immediately began to purr, and walked over to the table. Lola slipped onto the bench beside Eva, always pleased to be close to her. "It was a bit cold, but Pixey kept me warm," said Lola, still holding and stroking the half grown kitten.

"Do you know what day it is tomorrow?" asked The Magician.

"I can guess. We have been back about a week and there were ten days to sun-return when we left the Forest Castle," Lola replied.

"Yes, Lola, sun-return is upon us. I have never made too much of a spectacle of it since you came here, as I have wanted to let you just settle in and grow into your own gifts. This year, however, we need to mark it in a very special way and you will have to lead Eva and I in this."

"Me?" Lola now held Pixey very close and spoke through the fur on Pixey's neck. "What will I know that you two don't?"

"I have come to help explain that," said Eva. "It is time for you to learn the purpose of our Three Valleys in full."

"Purpose?" Lola was now confused. She never saw where she lived as having a purpose; it just was, like anywhere else.

"Yes," continued The Magician, "we are lucky that our land serves a great purpose to all other lands. It gives meaning to being here. So many in our insignificant world live without meaning. This causes so much suffering. Meaning of any kind of course has its roots in serving others; some say that is the only way to happiness. This can be looked at in many ways and is the subject of debate in all the courts and kingdoms of the world, but it comes down to one thing. Life has meaning when it is led genuinely for the good of humanity. Whether you are a King or a servant, this is a truth you cannot avoid."

"How do you know and how are we at the service of others?" asked Lola.

"Balance, we live in a balanced way. We do not take more than we give, whether it is to the land, the forest or each other," explained Eva. "All of the difficulties you have witnessed and been hurt by, Lola, over the last months, are because someone has tried to use power to take more than they need or understand. The serpents tried to take language and reasoning at the expense of others. The Serpent Lord tried to take you and your gifts. In the end, they could not succeed because they had taken something they didn't really need through greed, ignorance and a desire for power.

"We have in our kingdom centuries of wisdom that we guard to prove this. The wisdom is protected here. If we know that a set of these teachings is threatened by the people who hold it, we go and rescue it and bring it back here until we know it is safe to return it. Thus we are the caretakers of this wisdom."

"But where do we keep it?" asked Lola.

Pixey was now sitting between Lola and Eva, looking as if she was trying to keep up with the conversation. She could pick up the fascination in Lola's mind, but not quite the meaning.

The Magician smiled and stood up. He walked over to his bedroom door and opened it. Lola had only ever glimpsed inside his bedroom in the past. It was always his private space for his private study. It was a silent agreement between them.

The Magician now beckoned Lola towards himself, offering access to this private space. He made a specific gesture to the shelf above his bed. There, obviously collected over his life-time and perhaps also by those who went before him, was a collection of books in various condition, from fat volumes with gleaming gold spines to tattered scrolls.

"There, Lola," he said, "have you never wondered what all these books were for?"

"Oh," replied Lola, "I'm afraid I don't wonder about books very often."

Eva laughed. "That is what I suspected. The Magician can read and to some extent speak any language. The Forest Queen knew this, of course, which is why, when he was at the castle during the enchantment, the serpents dealt him such a hard blow. When the serpents took over the Forest Queen's body, they were to some extent able to use her knowledge. It was language they were most interested in controlling. Yet they had no idea that language's real purpose was to help us understand each other and the world around us, and to develop empathy."

"What's emptyith?" Lola struggled with the word.

"Being able to see the world from another's point of view, and valuing their experience as much as your own," The Magician explained. "Empathy," he repeated slowly.

"Empathy," Lola repeated. She looked at Pixey and then at the two adults. "How do you know you are feeling it?"

"You will have an experience of deep concern or appreciation for another," answered Eva.

Lola was quiet for a moment. She thought of all that had happened over the last few weeks. Some of it was too painful to really think about, especially the menacing Serpent Lord, and letting inklings of Oskar or Umir into her mind would make her feel deeply upset. She wondered how Henry and Sona felt now that they were reunited with Morgan and she wondered at the efforts that were made to rescue her on the cliffs.

"Do you think maybe you could feel it without knowing what it was?" Lola asked quietly.

"Oh yes." The Magician's voice was almost a whisper; he took Lola's hand. "Now," he said in a slightly more jovial voice, "some warm bread and honey. Anything else you would like me to magic up for your breakfast?"

The Magician had been doing much of the cooking. He got up and checked one of the side ovens that was warming a loaf of bread. He had left his bedroom door open so that his bookshelf was in Lola's view. All of those books contained all of the wisdom there was in the world. There they sat on that shelf, under their roof, and still Lola didn't know what to do with herself half of the time.

Hot tea, bread, honey and dried fruit were soon spread out on the table. A little goat's cheese had been made from Nanny's milk, though the milking was only just getting done. Lola made a mental note to put Nanny's milk to more use and make sure butter and cheese were made from it each week. The Magician just didn't have the same control over Nanny, and Nanny took advantage of that.

They sat in near-silence with Pixey, purring gently, next to Lola on the bench. Lola gave her a small saucer of Nanny's milk to keep her from being interested in the cheese.

Once everyone had had their fill, The Magician cleared his throat. "Well, now we must discuss what will happen at sun-return. I'm glad Pixey is here because she is an important part of this."

"Yes," continued Eva, "Isis will help her, but it is important that Pixey takes a major role. You must have the strongest of connections to stay grounded in what we are about to do."

Lola cautiously translated in her mind for Pixey as the others spoke. Pixey sat up straight, looking very important and sophisticated at the suggestion of taking part in something to help Lola.

"Are we going to sit together again in your meditation cave, Eva?" Lola asked as she gently stroked Pixey's back.

"Yes," answered Eva, "that will be a start, but it will be much more than that this time."

"All of these books and scrolls, Lola." The Magician turned to his room as he spoke and gestured towards his bookshelf. "They all must be hidden. They are the only complete versions of these texts perhaps anywhere in the world. If the Serpent Lord were to attack and these texts be found, who knows what might become of them? Books of wisdom can be used to control others; things can be taken out of context to satisfy the desire for power. Even worse, they could be completely disregarded or destroyed and then would be lost forever."

They were all silent for a moment. Even Lola was beginning to appreciate the significance of what was on the jagged oak shelf in The Magician's small whitewashed room.

"Shall we hide them in Eva's caves?" Lola asked quietly.

"No," replied Eva, "not even my caves are safe."

"They must be hidden in earth, water, fire and air," said The Magician. "They will sit in the throat of the dragon for safe keeping."

"Dragon?" whispered Lola. "You mean like the serpents but with wings like on Eva's mantle-piece?"

"Somewhat," The Magician said almost as quietly. "Dragons are not serpents, they are guardians of wisdom. Serpents are extremely intelligent, but they operate on our level. Though vast, their depth and influence is on the level of humans, only they dwell in the mirrors of our minds. They are that which we do not notice unless we look directly at ourselves. The dragon is his own complete universe. All the gross and subtle elements that the world is made up of are contained in the dragon. The dragon's understanding is beyond that of language. Every part of the landscape has his influence, whether a ridge for his spine, the mist for his breath, the sun's rays for his fire and the sun itself, his eye."

Lola's attention was glued to The Magician as he spoke. He paused for a moment as he noticed a focus from her that she had never shown him before.

"Are they only he's?" she asked quietly.

"Oh no," The Magician replied, "there are he's and she's. The one we will encounter is in fact a she. She has lived in the mountainside for centuries of centuries."

"Hundreds upon hundreds of years," Eva offered by way of explanation.

"How? I've never seen her," said Lola.

"She is now part of the mountain side. Dragons have many stages to their lives," said The Magician. "The final stage, once they have borne their young, is to become part of the landscape they have lived in. We dwell in this landscape and we pass by them every day. They make places sacred with their magic. It is where the wise can draw their power from. The greedy, evil and angry can misuse the power of a dragon, but they are then often consumed by the elements around them, which is part of the dragon's power. Our sacred pool is the entrance to her being and it is into her waterfall that we must venture with these texts."

"Won't they be ruined by the water?" asked Lola.

"We will wrap them all in oiled leather. They should be safe. It is what has been instructed," The Magician continued. "To be quite honest, I have no idea what will actually happen. The ritual has only been performed on a few occasions and not in my life-time. I only have the instructions of those who have gone before my grandfather."

Lola nodded her head, not really being able to imagine this plan working, but sure that the Magician did and that was what counted.

"I will have to take you through each step very carefully, Lola, before we actually do the ritual. Eva will wrap and load up the texts on Coal. You see it is you, Lola, the youngest, who must enter the throat of the dragon. We must be sure that every precaution is taken to have the same person, namely you, alive when they are to be retrieved."

"But how long will the books have to stay there?" asked Lola.

"We have no idea. When conflict enters the land, there may be a need to hide them for many years, perhaps beyond my life-time. Perhaps beyond even Eva's."

"How will we know when to go and get them?" Lola whispered, stunned by the thought of a time beyond The Magician's life.

"There will be signs and they will be clear. That is all I know," returned The Magician quietly.

Eva had stayed with them all day. She had helped prepare food to take up to her caves and oiled and wound strips of leather and hide around each book carefully. One book was left out. That was The Magician's own book of instructions. They were not spells, so to speak. Spells could only happen if the person making the spell was connected enough with magic to be part of the formula. The instructions told The Magician how to create the right conditions for Lola to connect with the power of the dragon. What would happen then was not detailed. Without the power to connect with the dragon, the instruction book was only an interesting set of rituals that would not be understood for what it really was.

Lola spent the day amerced in the book of

instructions with The Magician. "Think how you could call upon the elements of earth. What would that mean to you?" The Magician asked Lola.

Pixey sat attentively knowing that she must be Lola's anchor animal. Isis would support her, but it would be up to Pixey to keep Lola grounded.

By the time evening fell, Eva had loaded up Coal. Lola and Pixey were put in amongst the books and provisions on a makeshift saddle.

Lola looked at the cottage in the waning light. "Can I get stuck in the dragon?" she asked The Magician.

"There are instructions to call you out, should things go wrong, but the books might be lost. However, we will not lose you again, Lola." The Magician's voice was kind and reassuring.

"After this, can we just come back here and rest?"

"Of course, that is what winter is for." The Magician smiled as he tightened the straps on Lola's saddle.

Eva led the way up the path to her caves. She had a slight glow about her that lingered behind her, lighting the way for the others. Lola could see red streaks in the clouds behind the silhouetted trees.

Was this the dragon's fire? Lola thought, and the rocks and earth under Coal's hoofs, were these the dragon's bones? Suddenly everything, including the breeze on her face, became part of the dragon for Lola. It was as if she had been given the key to the whole world, which she now understood through the elements.

Coal was quiet, but Lola could tell he was sending

his warmth and kindness to both her and Pixey. It was as if he knew that they belonged in this great ritual and he took his part in it with honour and respect.

It seemed that they reached the caves quite quickly. Benu, Isis and Tara were waiting. There was the comforting smell of wood smoke from the slow burning stove in the kitchen cave. Lola had a moment of just yearning for a quiet evening, sitting by Eva's wood stove, sipping The Magician's soup and hearing stories, yet she now felt something pulling her, pulling her towards the path that led to the sacred pool. It was something much bigger than herself or Eva, or even The Magician.

"The way is too rocky for Coal, shall I get down?" suggested Lola.

"Yes, yes that would be helpful," replied The Magician, "but keep a hold of Pixey. Coal will have to negotiate the path very carefully and needs nothing else under his feet."

The Magician helped Pixey and Lola down. Eva took the satchel and pot that had been balancing on top of Coal's back with Pixey and Lola. The Magician carefully led Coal up the rocky path. There was a gentle co-operation between the man and the horse. The Magician gently showed Coal the next best place to put his hooves with a light that glowed about his hand. He stroked and reassured the horse with gentle pats on his neck and forehead as they made their way up to the ledge in front of Eva's caves.

CHAPTER 23

The Dragon

Eva was the first to reach the caves. In a moment each cave was lit up with a glow that welcomed the visitors to Eva's realm.

"Come." She beckoned towards her kitchen cave as Lola and Pixey reached the top ledge.

Isis was waiting at the entrance, impatient to sniff and lick Pixey over. The minute Lola put Pixey down Isis went over to her and rigorously washed her with the same roughness that Sophie used.

"*Careful,*" warned Benu, "*connect with her, don't frighten her off.*"

Pixey wasn't frightened, just annoyed at Isis's display of dominance. She knew she didn't always wash behind her ears or preen her whiskers as well as she should, but there was no need for Isis to make a point of it.

Isis suddenly stopped. She then sniffed Pixey all over and gave her a thump on the nose with her paw. "*You'll do,*" Isis sent as she sauntered away to the fire where she sat down to wash her own paws, but kept eying Pixey to be sure she was doing the right thing.

"Come and have a warm drink before we start," Eva said to Lola. Eva was now brewing tea over her wood stove. "There is a lot of goodness in this. It will sustain you and keep you warm."

Eva handed Lola a small steaming mug. Lola sniffed and then sipped cautiously. It was bitter. She took another small sip. Bitter, but not unpleasant. Lola continued to slowly sip and felt the hot liquid seep down through her body, warming her deeply. She looked on as Pixey continued to be inspected. She didn't quite know how to help. Eva noticed her concern.

"Keep drinking, Lola. They will work it out for themselves."

The Magician now entered the kitchen cave. "Coal is ready, I've put fleece around his legs for warmth. It should hold if he needs to go into the water."

Water, thought Lola. What would it be like going into the water at this time of year? Surely the sacred pool would be frozen over.

Eva handed The Magician a mug of the tea as well. They all sipped in silence. All were quietly settling into themselves, gently looking at each other, privately anticipating what was about to happen.

Their mugs were empty now. The Magician smiled. "Time to go and find the dragon, I think," he said quietly.

Eva stood up and led the way out and into her meditation cave. The candles were already lit. Cushions were set out for each of them. Isis was herding Pixey into form by nudging her towards Lola's cushion and then regally sitting on Eva's. Benu went to sit near The Magician's cushions. Tara sat at the door.

"We will simply start with ourselves. Lola, sit with Pixey in meditation and find out who you are just now, then Eva will lead us to where we need to be, that is until it is your turn to take the lead." The Magician was sitting on his cushion now with Benu draped across his lap.

Eva rang her bell. Lola was still wondering about what might happen and looking around the cave when she felt Eva's and The Magician's immediate inward focus at the sound. Benu and Isis sat as sentinels on their laps.

Lola stroked Pixey. *"This is us,"* Lola sent, *"we must go with them."* Then, as if it had been the most natural thing she had ever done, Pixey collected herself up and focused inward; Lola followed suit.

Pixey seemed to quickly lead Lola inward to the place where Lola had been all those weeks ago - to the open pasture. This time the sky was filled with stars, more stars than Lola had ever seen in the night sky before. There was one, very strong, arching line of stars. Lola was captivated by its beauty.

"The Draco." Lola heard her mother's voice. It was so like Eva's, but with a slightly lower echo all of its own. "These stars show the dragon in space. The dragon is everywhere. You must become one with the dragon."

Lola stood up. Pixey settled on Lola's cushion, her little self being so small, but her inner strength now felt like that of a panther. She stayed on the spot where Lola had been sitting, keeping part of Lola grounded in the cave.

Lola left the cave. She could smell Coal's soft breath in the freezing air. She took the halter gently in her hand and started down the path towards the sacred pool.

As Lola passed her rowan tree it bowed to her. She acknowledged this with a slight nod of her head. She then went on. Gently, reverently, she treaded the path to the pool. Crystals of frozen air tickled her face. The cold felt welcoming. It gave her heart a lift while deepening her focus.

Coal easily negotiated the path, even with his heavy load. It was as if something or someone else was ferrying and softening their way.

The Magician and Eva followed. They did not know if their presence would hinder Lola's task, but curiosity drove them just as much as concern for her safety.

When Lola reached the pool, there was already a slight golden glow coming across the surface reflected from the frozen waterfall.

Lola stood before the pool. *"Shall I bring the wisdom to you?"* she asked in her mind, having no doubt that she was now standing before the dragon. The waterfall glowed more brightly. At first Lola could hear the gentle trickle of water, then the sound of running water. The glow of the ice now intensified and then the frozen waterfall broke away with a great gush. Ice, water and fire were all fusing. Hues of orange, blue and green swirled around the pool as the great mass of an iceberg emerged from the gushing waterfall. The iceberg shot towards the shore where Lola stood and then slowed to a gentle glide as it reached her. It settled against the frozen sand, making a crunching sound as it came to a halt.

Lola knelt down and touched the iceberg as she had touched the water on her previous visit. It quivered slightly, but gave off a sense of benevolence that reassured her. The iceberg was big enough to lead Coal onto. *"Shall I put the wisdom here?"* She looked up at the glowing waterfall.

"You must come too," a clear deep voice echoed in Lola's mind.

Lola turned to Coal and reached again for his halter. Coal was ready to oblige, although he had no desire to enter the icy waters even afloat on an iceberg.

"Alone," the voice rang again in Lola's mind. This time it sent a chill through to her gut. She could feel Pixey, back in the cave, trying to hold her and tugging at her heart. Lola looked at the waterfall and then sent to Pixey, *"I can do this Little Three, my dear Pixey Chandra. Keep hold of me - I'll stay with you."*

Pixey readjusted her focus. She knew she had to hang on and let go at the same time. Both she and Lola felt more comfortable now.

Lola began to unload all of the wisdom texts onto the iceberg. As she pulled apart the packs that had been carefully constructed some of the oiled leather started to pull away. Each text had a slight glow, though they were different colours. The colours of the dragon, thought Lola.

The Magician and Eva continued to watch from further up the path. Lola was skillfully building a pyramid, fitting each book into her intricate construction. It began to glow with the white light of the iceberg.

Finally Coal's back was unloaded. He stepped away and warm, sweet mist came from his nostrils. Lola affectionately stroked his nose and then turned and faced the waterfall. White light glowed behind it.

"*Come now,*" the voice echoed in her mind. Lola stepped onto the iceberg, having to steady herself slightly.

Eva took a step towards the pool. The Magician held Eva's arm. "Have faith," he said. "She's more than equipped to do this, just send her love and courage. Physical separation from her is meaningless at the moment." Eva stopped herself at The Magician's words.

Lola's small form was silhouetted against the pyramid of the glowing wisdom texts. She faced the gushing waterfall, not looking back, knowing symbolically that that might bring her commitment into question. The iceberg slid through the water silently. It stopped in front of the waterfall. Lola looked straight through it. Yes, the cavern tunnel on the other side looked exactly like the throat of a gigantic animal of some kind. She felt Pixey adjusting to these new sensations. Then the iceberg lurched forward. Lola was through the waterfall. There was a moment of freezing spray and then intense heat. Her senses could barely register what was happening and she looked around feeling disorientated and frightened.

"Stay calm, look ahead, you must go forward." It was Pixey's little voice. Pixey, now with Benu and Isis, was creating a rope-like connection in Lola's mind to keep her from getting lost.

Lola looked ahead. The tunnel was made of fire. Surely both she and the books would be burnt to a crisp if they carried on, she thought. Yet, the iceberg slid through the tunnel, still intact. Lola could still feel the frozen ice beneath her boots, while the top of her body began to sweat from the intense heat of the tunnel.

A deep voice seemed to hum or purr as the iceberg slid onto dry rock. Lola stepped off the ice onto dry land. Now warmth could be felt through her boots. Eva's love now started to penetrate through Lola. Eva, who Lola now knew had stood on this spot before her, in years past.

Then Lola heard Eva's voice. *"Face forward, not back and do not flinch. The flames cannot burn you if you completely let go. Pixey will keep you safe."*

Lola now felt all three cats; Benu and Isis had joined Pixey on the same cushion. She could also feel Eva and The Magician. Yet, this great being, whom she stood at the mercy of, wanted her attention. It wanted her to give it her complete and utter focus.

Lola turned towards the depths of the tunnel. The wisdom texts were scattered about her feet. The iceberg had evaporated behind her. She looked up, lifted her arms and opened the depth of her heart towards the flaming tunnel.

"Protect these sacred texts so that in the future human beings will have the guidance they need," she spoke into the tunnel.

Upon her words, a wall of flames came shooting towards her. The heat was searing, yet it didn't burn. Lola stood fast, opening her heart, stretching out her arms. The wind of the tunnel rushed past her. She closed her eyes to shield them from the intense light. She could smell the leather and paper burning. For a second, she felt panic at the texts being destroyed, but she held fast – surely, she thought, this was meant to happen.

The sound of the flames shooting past her was like thunder, only it was continuous. Lola felt her head pounding, wondering if the pressure of the wind and the heat would make her explode. She tried to hold fast, willing her legs to support her whilst her arms continued to embrace the inferno. Doubt in her own strength momentarily seeped into her mind. Immediately the flames stopped. Lola collapsed on the now empty stone floor of the cave.

"You nearly proved yourself, but there was a moment of doubt," purred the deep voice of the cavern.

Lola tried to bring herself to her feet, stumbling on her shaking legs. "Have I failed?" she whispered into the darkness.

"Failure was never an option. You will be tested further until you succeed. You will enter the mountain and face

whatever fears you still have armed only with this."

Abruptly from the tunnel a white light shone. Lola again had to shield her eyes, but in the middle of the stone ground before her she could see a large ruby crystal. From it emanated a glow that began to penetrate Lola. It gave an air of confidence, positivity and courage, as if it was already part of her. She walked towards it and carefully picked it up.

The crystal was smooth, except for a few rough edges, but it was an irregular shape. It was the same temperature as Lola's body. As she handled it, she felt her own body start to glow. The light in the tunnel disappeared as quickly as it had appeared.

"Walk on," the voice said.

Lola reverently held the crystal in both hands and ventured forward. The tunnel was of a smooth but slightly wet stone. It had ripple patterns that might, she suspected, reflect what the throat of a real dragon would look like on the inside. Lola had to remind herself that it was in fact the throat of a dragon, but in a form humans did not expect to find. Its red and gray rippled pattern would be common on the walls of many caves. Perhaps all caves lead to the stomach of a dragon, she thought. Lola knew this was where she was now going.

The tunnel continued in a straight line with a slight decline. All the while the crystal glowed, lighting the passage efficiently enough to make the way visible, but not enough to reveal the full view of the walls and the ceiling of the tunnel.

Lola walked on as if in a dreamlike state. She had no thought of anything in the outside world now. She only sought the dragon. She was pulled along by the glow of the crystal and plunged deeper into the soul of the dragon as well as delving deeper into her own power.

The further down Lola went, the closer her heart felt to the dragon's heart. She felt the beat pulsing through her own. The light of the crystal now pulsed with the beating of these two hearts. As Lola came to the end of the tunnel and entered a great chamber, she could feel fresh, freezing air. The pulsing now became as loud as a drum beat. The slow intentional rhythm was beating through Lola's body. She stopped; with eyes closed, she relished the slow steady rhythm, rocking and soothing her whole being.

"What makes you think you can hold the heart of the dragon?" The voice was a high-pitched growl and it startled Lola out of her trance-like state. It was so unlike the smooth deep voice that had previously emanated from the tunnel.

Lola looked around. Sitting on the ground a few feet away from her was a creature with the head of a tattered crow and the body of a lizard. It had disheveled feathers growing out of its elbows. The creature had a pile of small stones in front of it. Lola looked at them, curiously wondering what the purpose of collecting such common stones might be.

"Don't think you are going to have my precious gems," the creature scolded. "They are mine, not yours, you filthy little thief. Stealing away from the castle, that kitten, not yours, the dog, not yours and all those people, stealing away their hearts, but you don't care. You are worthless - worth nothing! And now you hold that precious stone thinking it is yours. But it is mine! Mine!"

High-pitched growls and threats started to echo all over the cavern. The creature wrapped one wing-like arm around its hoard of stones and started trying to swipe the crystal from Lola's hands with the other. Each time she tried to step back the creature seemed to advance towards her without having to move itself.

Lola looked back at the tunnel. It was dark. She turned to use the glow of the crystal to light a way out, but every time she did, the glow disappeared for a second and then the creature was before her again.

"Don't you turn your back on me!" it shrieked. But Lola kept trying to back away and shift from its path, all the while becoming more disorientated.

Then Lola stopped. A wave of calm descended into her. She remembered one of The Magician's favourite stories. It was a story of two holy men wandering in a great forest, contemplating and reflecting. Two bandits came upon these men and, as the men had no belongings to steal, the bandits decided to kill them instead. One holy man became filled with terror and started to climb a tree to find safety. The other simply bowed his neck to let the bandit kill him. The first bandit was so terrified by this act of selflessness that he screamed and ran up a tree himself while the other bandit ran into the forest.

Lola looked at the creature. It wasn't as big as her. It chattered away to itself as saliva dripped from its beak-like mouth and its red eyes twitched. She pitied it as well as being repulsed by it. It was as if hate and greed had been wrapped up in flesh and bone and then left to rot in the stomach of this cavern, collecting stones as though they were the only things of value to collect.

"Very well," Lola tried to say kindly, "have the crystal."

The creature grabbed the crystal and as it did so there was an explosion of light as it touched its hands. Lola crouched down, shielding her face and eyes with her arm.

A soft white light started to enter the tunnel. The air was filled with a fine white dust. Lola stood up slowly and looked around. The creature lay lifeless, curled around its pile of stones. Next to it lay a necklace of ruby crystals glowing softly. Lola picked it up carefully, trying to avoid contact with the creature. The necklace was warm. She could feel a tiny pulse going through it. She gently placed it around her neck. The necklace dissolved into her skin in an instant and the body of the creature dissolved into white light, leaving behind only a dim glow.

Now Lola heard a gurgling sound coming from deep in the cavern, then a bubbling. She looked down. Water was seeping across the patterned rock floor around her feet and now into her boots. Her toes were wet, but the water was warm - not like the nearly frozen water in the sacred pool. Suddenly a whooshing drowned out all of the gurgling and bubbling and Lola saw a wall of turbulent water coming towards her with a blue glow all of its own. It was too late to run. The wall of water crashed into Lola and she found herself being swept along by the torrent back up the tunnel she had come through. The water was still warm and she was completely submerged. She knew she shouldn't fight it, but should just go with it. She tried to keep the same steady frame of mind as she had when the flames had rushed past her, but this time she would not doubt herself. She readied herself for the plunge into the freezing water of the sacred pool, which she knew the torrent was going to throw her into.

"Pixey - send to The Magician. I will need him," Lola sent as calmly as she could.

Pixey was still focusing inward on her cushion. She could have pulled back Lola at any time, but she sensed Lola would reconnect when the time was right. It had been challenging and testing, but they seemed to be nearing success.

"He's already there," Pixey sent back with a purr.

At that precise moment Eva and The Magician reached into the freezing pool, each taking one of Lola's arms. For a moment they could see the glow of the ruby necklace.

"She has done it," The Magician exclaimed softly as he met Eva's eyes, which brimmed with relief and pride.

The glow of the waterfall stopped. The sound of

the waterfall stopped, and it froze over.

The Magician wrapped Lola in his cloak as he pulled her close. As her feet came free of the pool, the pool froze.

"Come." He gently lifted Lola onto Coal's back. "I'm sure Eva's fires are ready to warm you."

And they were, but Lola wasn't feeling the cold. Warmth kindled now within her, but she was wet and hoped that Eva would have some dry clothing. They made their way back up the path.

The night was clear and frozen. Layers of stars inhabited the sky, more than Lola could ever remember. She scanned the sky curiously. Then, there it was, shining more brightly than she had ever noticed – the diamond studded arch of the Draco constellation. She would never miss it again, she promised herself.

Lola looked back now at the dim glow from the pool. She felt a sudden surge of love and respect for the dragon. It was remarkable how safe she had felt inside it. Now it was as if she was part of the dragon and the dragon was part of her. She almost felt a longing to be close to it. She would go and sit by the pool soon and see if that deep soothing voice would speak to her again.

Eva's sleeping cave had a fire lit and, true to Eva's caring nature, there was a warm red robe to put over a freshly cleaned shift for Lola. There were also soft knitted socks and a shawl.

"I'll dry these in the other cave, Lola." Eva was helping her pull the shawl up over her shoulders in the most natural of ways, as women who are sisters or the like often do. "I'll bring Pixey and a hot drink back. Get in bed, Lola, you must reflect on what has happened. There is no need to talk about it or explain it until you are sure that would be useful to you."

Lola said very little. She smiled and nodded and gladly received her hot drink and Pixey a few minutes later.

"The Magician and I will go back to meditate and finish this long night, but you two must rest. Sleep, sleep deeply my dear." Eva gently stroked Lola's forehead as she spoke and then softly kissed it before she went out.

Pixey was prodding and purring on Lola's chest. She finally settled down, resting her chin on Lola's breastbone and both fell deeply asleep.

Lola was now back in the clothes, which had been hanging in front of the fire. It was well before dawn, but the stars had changed position. Clouds had begun to gather on the Eastern ridge. Lola was noticing more about the weather and the four directions and the paths of stars and the moon. Things that The Magician often commented on, but never formally taught her.

Pixey was being lightly inspected by Isis again. This time a bit more respect was paid. Benu looked on with amusement at Isis who was having to give Pixey credit for how well she had stabilized Lola during the journey inside the dragon. They had had little work to do in supporting her.

Isis licked Pixey on the forehead and then sat and looked at her. *"I suppose you'll be up again at some point."* Isis sent to Pixey. *"You passed the test. You and Lola will always do this together now, whenever the sun and moon are doing something interesting."*

Pixey smiled with her eyes, almost shyly, but thought to herself, *"I didn't know it had anything to do with the sun and moon. I shall have to ask Lola about that later."*

"Come Pixey," Lola called. She crouched down and gave Isis and Benu a quick stroke on the forehead each. She then scooped up Pixey and nestled the kitten into her shawl for the ride home. *"Look, we get special treatment. Coal is our ride back down."*

Pixey was already settling in and stretching one paw out to relax her right shoulder and head against Lola.

The Magician helped them onto Coal. Eva waved goodbye from her ledge. Lola wished Eva would come down with them. Eva said she would in a day or two.

As they started to make their way down the path, snow began to gently fall. Again, in the distance Lola could hear the howling of wolves, as if they were telling a continuing story. They howled of a girl who tamed the serpents and who could stand in the throat of the dragon and bear the heat of the flames. This girl had taken the sacred treasure into the dragon, to hide it from the armies of the Serpent Lord.

Yet, there was sadness in the depth of her heart. She had a lost faithful friend. This friend had protected her in the dungeons of the Serpent Lord's palace, and had helped her escape. None of what she had just done, could have been done without him.

This friend, they promised to find, and return to her.

Acknowledgements

Once again I would like to thank family and friends for their support and encouragement in bringing this next book into the world, especially my dear friend Donna. I also want to thank Otto and Leo for their inspiration in helping me create Lance and Oskar respectively, and reminding me that the world can be a wonderful place.

About the author

Elizabeth Scott grew up in New England, but has lived her adult life in England. She is inspired by the natural world of both her childhood, especially woodland, and the British landscape. She lives in Sussex with her husband and two cats, all of whom wander through her stories from time to time.

Postscript

It is my intention as a writer to create a world where the reader will want to stay and dwell awhile rather than a world where they will wish the characters a safe exit. It is also my intention outside of writing to help create a world where children are safe and the natural world can thrive. Therefore, 10% of the net profit from this book, and others that follow, will go to charities that support wildlife conservation and child welfare. If you have enjoyed it, please tell two friends.